THOUSAND
CRANES

BOOKS BY

Yasunari Kawabata

THOUSAND CRANES

SNOW COUNTRY

THOUSAND
CRANES

YASUNARI KAWABATA

Translated by

EDWARD G. SEIDENSTICKER

CHARLES E. TUTTLE COMPANY
Suido 1-chome, 2-6, Bunkyo-ku, Tokyo

UNESCO COLLECTION OF REPRESENTATIVE WORKS

Japanese Series

This book has been accepted in the Japanese Series of the Translations Collection of the United Nations Educational, Scientific and Cultural Organization (UNESCO).

Originally published in Japanese as *Sembazuru*

Published by the Charles E. Tuttle Company, Inc., of Rutland, Vermont and Tokyo, Japan, with editorial offices at Suido 1-chome, 2-6, Bunkyo-ku, Tokyo, Japan, by special arrangement with Alfred A. Knopf, Inc., New York.

First Tuttle edition, 1967
Twentieth printing, 1996

PRINTED IN JAPAN

A Note on the Tea Ceremony, the Backdrop for This Novel

THE BEGINNINGS of the tea cult can be traced to the thirteenth century and the beginnings of Zen Buddhism in Japan. Early Zen masters recommended tea as the beverage most excellent for cultivating the spirit, and in the centuries that followed, an elaborate symbolism and a carefully contrived ritual encouraged the Zen disciple in his aim to achieve imperturbability. Rustic utensils and surroundings were brought into harmony to remind him of the Buddhahood in a clod of earth, and the withdrawn repose of the cottage and its garden turned his mind to the permanent behind the ephemeral—to the intersection of time and eternity. If the quiet and restraint of the ideal tea ceremony are somewhat lacking in ceremonies described in this novel, Mr. Kawabata's characters nonetheless seem to pause at the intersection, marked for them by the permanence of the old tea vessels and the impermanence of the owners.

The tea ceremony is a stylized way of preparing tea from water heated over a charcoal hearth. The smallest detail, from the charcoal to the receptacle for left-over water, must be carefully planned.

The host pours water from an iron kettle into a handleless cup—here translated "bowl" because it is considerably larger than an ordinary teacup—adds powdered tea, and stirs with a bamboo whisk until an appropriate layer of foam has accumulated. The guest drinks according to a prescribed form and returns the bowl. That, on the surface, is all; but to the initiated the details of the cottage, the utensils, and the performance have given something more—perhaps only an impression of affluence, perhaps a sense of timelessness.

Contents

Drawings by Fumi Komatsu

THOUSAND
CRANES

❧ ❧ ❧

Thousand Cranes

EVEN WHEN he reached Kamakura and the Engakuji Temple, Kikuji did not know whether or not he would go to the tea ceremony. He was already late.

He received an announcement whenever Kurimoto Chikako offered tea at the inner cottage of the Engakuji. He had not once gone since his father's death, however. He thought of the announcements as no more than formal gestures in memory of his father.

This time there had been a postscript: she wanted him to meet a young lady to whom she was giving tea lessons.

As he read it, Kikuji thought of Chikako's birthmark.

Had he been eight, perhaps, or nine? He had been taken by his father to visit Chikako, and they had found her in the breakfast room. Her kimono was open. She was cutting the hair on her birthmark with a small pair of scissors. It covered half the left breast and ran down into the hollow between the breasts, as large as the palm of one's hand. Hair seemed to be growing on the purple-black mark, and Chikako was in process of cutting it.

"You brought the boy with you?"

In surprise, she snatched at the neck of her kimono. Then, perhaps because haste only complicated her efforts to cover herself, she turned slightly away and carefully tucked kimono into obi.

The surprise must have been less at Kikuji's father than at Kikuji. Since a maid had met them at the door, Chikako must have known at least that Kikuji's father had come.

Kikuji's father did not go into the breakfast room. He sat down in the next room instead, the room where Chikako gave lessons.

"Do you suppose I could have a cup of tea?" Kikuji's father asked absently. He looked up at the hanging in the alcove.

"Yes." But Chikako did not move.

On the newspaper at her knee, Kikuji had seen hairs like whiskers.

Though it was broad daylight, rats were scurrying about in the hollow ceiling. A peach tree was in bloom near the veranda.

When at length she took her place by the tea hearth, Chikako seemed preoccupied.

Some ten days later, Kikuji heard his mother telling his father, as if it were an extraordinary secret of which he could not have known, that Chikako was unmarried because of the birthmark. There was compassion in her eyes.

"Oh?" Kikuji's father nodded in apparent surprise. "But it wouldn't matter, would it, if her husband were to see it? Especially if he knew of it before he married her?"

"That's exactly what I said to her. But after all a woman is a woman. I don't think I would ever be able to tell a man that I had a big mark on my breast."

"But she's hardly young any more."

"Still it wouldn't be easy. A man with a birthmark could probably get married and just laugh when he was found out."

"Did you see the mark?"

"Don't be silly. Of course not."

"You just talked about it?"

"She came for my lesson, and we talked about all sorts of things. I suppose she felt like confessing."

Kikuji's father was silent.

"Suppose she were to marry. What would the man think?"

"He'd probably be disgusted by it. But he might find something attractive in it, in having it for a secret. And then again the defect might bring out good points. Anyway, it's hardly a problem worth worrying about."

"I told her it was no problem at all. But it's on the breast, she says."

"Oh?"

"The hardest thing would be having a child to nurse. The husband might be all right, but the child."

"The birthmark would keep milk from coming?"

"Not that. No, the trouble would be having the

child look at the birthmark while it was nursing. I hadn't seen quite so far myself, but a person who actually has a birthmark thinks of these things. From the day it was born it would drink there; and from the day it began to see, it would see that ugly mark on its mother's breast. Its first impression of the world, its first impression of its mother, would be that ugly birthmark, and there the impression would be, through the child's whole life."

"Oh? But isn't that inventing worries?"

"You could nurse it on cow's milk, I suppose, or hire a wet nurse."

"I should think the important thing would be whether or not there was milk, not whether or not there was a birthmark."

"I'm afraid not. I actually wept when I heard. So that's how it is, I thought. I wouldn't want our Kikuji nursing at a breast with a birthmark on it."

"Oh?"

At this show of ingenuousness, a wave of indignation came over Kikuji, and a wave of resentment at his father, who could ignore him even though he too had seen the mark.

Now, however, almost twenty years later, Kikuji was able to smile at the thought of his father's confusion.

From the time he was ten or so, he often thought of his mother's words and started with uneasiness at the idea of a half-brother or half-sister sucking at the birthmark.

It was not just fear of having a brother or sister born away from home, a stranger to him. It was rather fear of that brother or sister in particular. Kikuji was obsessed with the idea that a child who sucked at that breast, with its birthmark and its hair, must be a monster.

Chikako appeared to have had no children. One could, if one wished, suspect that his father had not allowed her to. The association of birthmark and baby that had saddened his mother might have been his father's device for convincing Chikako that she did not want children. In any case, Chikako produced none, either while Kikuji's father lived or after his death.

Perhaps Chikako had made her confession so soon after Kikuji had seen the birthmark because she feared that Kikuji himself would tell of it.

Chikako did not marry. Had the birthmark then governed her whole life?

Kikuji never forgot the mark. He could sometimes imagine even that his own destinies were enmeshed in it.

When he received the note saying that Chikako meant to make the tea ceremony her excuse for introducing him to a young lady, the birthmark once more floated before him; and, since the introduction would be made by Chikako, he wondered if the young lady herself would have a perfect skin, a skin unmarred by so much as a dot.

Had his father occasionally squeezed the birthmark between his fingers? Had he even bitten at it? Such were Kikuji's fantasies.

Even now, as he walked through the temple grounds and heard the chirping of birds, those were the fantasies that came to him.

Some two or three years after the incident, Chikako had somehow turned masculine in manner. Now she was quite sexless.

At the ceremony today she would be bustling about energetically. Perhaps that breast with its birthmark would have withered. Kikuji felt a smile of relief come to his lips; and just then two young women hurried up behind him.

He stopped to let them pass.

"Do you know whether the cottage Miss Kurimoto has taken might be in this direction?" he asked.

"Yes, it is," the two answered in unison.

Kikuji already knew, and he could have told from their dress that they were on their way to a tea ceremony. He had asked because he had to make it clear to himself that he was going.

One of the girls was beautiful. She carried a bundle wrapped in a kerchief, the thousand-crane pattern in white on a pink crape background.

. 2 .

The two girls were changing to fresh *tabi*[1] when Kikuji arrived.

He looked in from behind them. The main room was a large one, some eight mats in area.[2]

Even so, the guests presented a solid row of knees. There seemed to be only women, women in bright kimonos.

Chikako saw him immediately. As if in surprise, she stood up to greet him.

"Come in, come in. What a prize! Please, it will be quite all right to come in from there." She pointed to the sliding door at the upper end of the room, before the alcove.

Kikuji flushed. He felt the eyes of all those women.

"Ladies only, is it?"

"We did have a gentleman earlier, but he left. You are the one bright spot."

"Hardly bright."

---

[1] Short split-toed socks.
[2] A mat is about one yard by two.

"Oh, certainly, you have all the qualifications. The one spot of scarlet."

Kikuji waved his hand to indicate that he would prefer a less conspicuous door.

The young lady was wrapping her discarded *tabi* in the thousand-crane kerchief. She stood aside to let him pass.

The anteroom was cluttered with boxes of sweets, tea utensils brought by Chikako, and bundles that belonged to the guests. In the far corner a maid was washing something.

Chikako came in.

"Well, what do you think of her? A nice girl, isn't she?"

"The one with the thousand-crane kerchief?"

"Kerchief? How would I know about kerchiefs? The one who was standing here, the pretty one. She's the Inamura girl."

Kikuji nodded vaguely.

"Kerchief. What odd things you notice. A person can't be too careful. I thought you had come together. I was delighted."

"What are you talking about?"

"You met on the way. It's a sign of a bond between you. And your father knew Mr. Inamura."

"Oh?"

"The family had a raw-silk business in Yokohama. She knows nothing about today. You can look her over at your leisure."

Chikako's voice was no small one, and Kikuji was in an agony of apprehension lest she be heard through the paper-paneled door that separated them from the main party. Suddenly she brought her face close to his.

"But there's a complication." She lowered her voice. "Mrs. Ota is here, and her daughter with her." She studied Kikuji's expression. "I didn't invite her. But it's been the rule that anyone who happens to be in the neighborhood can drop in. The other day I even had some Americans. I'm sorry, but what am I to do when she gets wind of an affair? Of course she doesn't know about you and the Inamura girl."

"About me and the Inamura girl? But I . . ." Kikuji wanted to say that he had not come prepared for a *miai*, a meeting the announced purpose of which was to view a prospective bride. Somehow the words would not come. His throat muscles stiffened.

"But Mrs. Ota is the one who should be uncomfortable. You can pretend that nothing is wrong."

Chikako's way of dismissing the matter annoyed him.

Her intimacy with his father had evidently been of short duration. For the rest of his father's life, however, Chikako made herself useful in his house. She would come to help in the kitchen when there was to be a tea ceremony and even when ordinary guests were expected.

The idea that Kikuji's mother should begin feeling jealous of a sexless Chikako seemed funny, worth only a wry smile. No doubt his mother came to sense that his father had seen the birthmark, but the storm had passed; and Chikako, as if she too had quite forgotten, became his mother's companion.

In the course of time Kikuji too came to treat her lightly. As he turned his childish tantrums on her, the suffocating revulsion of his younger days seemed to fade.

It was perhaps an appropriate life for Chikako, that she had lapsed into sexlessness and been made a convenient fixture.

With Kikuji's family her base, she was modestly successful as an instructor in the tea ceremony.

Kikuji even felt a certain faint sympathy for her when, upon his father's death, it came to him that she had repressed the woman in her after that one brief, fleeting affair.

The hostility of Kikuji's mother, moreover, was held in check by the question of Mrs. Ota.

After the death of Ota, who had been a companion in the pursuit of tea, Kikuji's father had undertaken to dispose of Ota's tea utensils, and he had thus been drawn to the widow.

Chikako hastened to inform Kikuji's mother.

Chikako of course became his mother's ally—indeed a too hard-working ally. She prowled after his father, she frequently went to threaten Mrs. Ota. All her own latent jealousy seemed to explode.

Kikuji's quiet, introspective mother, taken aback at this flaming intervention, worried rather about what people might think.

Even in front of Kikuji, Chikako would berate Mrs. Ota, and when his mother showed signs of displeasure, Chikako would say that it did Kikuji no harm to hear.

"And the time before, too, when I went to have it out with her, there was the child, listening to everything. I ask you, didn't I all of a sudden hear sniffling in the next room?"

"A girl?" Kikuji's mother frowned.

"Yes. Eleven years old, I believe Mrs. Ota said. Really, there is something wrong with that woman. I thought she would scold the girl for eavesdropping, and what did she do but get up and bring her in, and sit holding her, right there in front of me. I suppose she needed a supporting actor to help with the sobbing."

"But don't you think it's a little sad for the child?"

"That's exactly why we should use the child to get back at her. The child knows everything. I must say that it's a pretty child, though. A round little face." Chikako looked at Kikuji. "Suppose we have Kikuji here speak to his father."

"Try not to spread the poison too far, if you don't mind." Even Kikuji's mother had to protest.

"You keep the poison damned up inside you, that's the whole trouble. Pull yourself together; spit it all out. See how thin you are, and she all plump and glowing. There really is something not right about her—she thinks that if she weeps pathetically enough, everyone will understand. And right there in the room where she sees Mr. Mitani, she has a picture of her own husband on exhibit. I'm surprised Mr. Mitani hasn't spoken to her about it."

And, after the death of Kikuji's father, this Mrs. Ota came to Chikako's tea ceremony and even brought her daughter.

Kikuji felt the touch of something cold.

Chikako said that she had not invited Mrs. Ota today. Still it was astonishing: the two women had been seeing each other since his father's death. Perhaps even the daughter was taking tea lessons.

"If it bothers you, I might ask her to leave." Chikako looked into his eyes.

"It makes no difference to me. Of course, if she wants to go . . ."

"If she were a person who thought of such things, she wouldn't have brought so much unhappiness to your father and mother."

"The daughter is with her?" Kikuji had never seen the daughter.

It seemed wrong to meet the girl of the thousand cranes here before Mrs. Ota. And he was even more repelled at the thought of meeting the daughter today.

But Chikako's voice clawed at his ear and scraped at his nerves. "Well, she will know I'm here. I can't run away now." He stood up.

He went in through the door by the alcove, and took his place at the upper end of the room.

Chikako followed close after him. "This is Mr. Mitani. Old Mr. Mitani's son." Her tone was most formal.

Kikuji made his bow, and as he raised his head he had a clear view of the daughter. Somewhat flustered, he had at first not distinguished one lady from another in the bright flood of kimonos. He saw now that Mrs. Ota was directly opposite him.

"Kikuji." It was Mrs. Ota. Her voice, audible throughout the room, was frankly affectionate. "I haven't written in so long. And it's been so very long since I last saw you." She tugged at the daughter's sleeve, urging her to be quick with her greetings. The daughter flushed and looked at the floor.

To Kikuji this was indeed odd. He could not detect the faintest suggestion of hostility in Mrs. Ota's manner. She seemed wholly warm, tender, overcome with pleasure at an unexpected meeting. One could only conclude that she was wholly unaware of her place in the assembly.

The daughter sat stiffly, with bowed head.

At length noticing, Mrs. Ota, too, flushed. She still looked at Kikuji, however, as if she wanted to rush to his side, or as if there were things she must say to him. "You are studying tea, then, are you?"

"I know nothing at all about it."

"Really? But you have it in your blood." Her emotions seemed too much for her. Her eyes were moist.

Kikuji had not seen her since his father's funeral. She had hardly changed in four years.

The white neck, rather long, was as it had been, and the full shoulders that strangely matched the slender neck—it was a figure young for her years. The mouth and nose were small in proportion to the eyes. The little nose, if one bothered to notice, was cleanly modeled and most engaging. When she spoke, her lower lip was thrust forward a little, as if in a pout.

The daughter had inherited the long neck and the full shoulders. Her mouth was larger, however, and tightly closed. There was something almost funny about the mother's tiny lips beside the daughter's.

Sadness clouded the girl's eyes, darker than her mother's.

Chikako poked at the embers in the hearth. "Miss Inamura, suppose you make tea for Mr. Mitani. I don't believe you've had your turn yet."

The girl of the thousand cranes stood up.

Kikuji had noticed her beside Mrs. Ota.

He had avoided looking at her, however, once he had seen Mrs. Ota and the daughter.

Chikako was of course showing the girl off for his inspection.

When she had taken her place at the hearth, she turned to Chikako.

"And which bowl shall I use?"

"Let me see. The Oribe[3] should do," Chikako answered. "It belonged to Mr. Mitani's father. He was very fond of it, and he gave it to me."

Kikuji remembered the tea bowl Chikako had placed before the girl. It had indeed belonged to his father, and his father had received it from Mrs. Ota.

And what of Mrs. Ota, seeing at the ceremony today a bowl that had been treasured by her dead husband and passed from Kikuji's father to Chikako?

Kikuji was astounded at Chikako's tactlessness.

[3] A Seto ware dating from the sixteenth century.

But one could not avoid concluding that Mrs. Ota, too, showed a certain want of tact.

Here, making tea for him, clean against the rankling histories of the middle-aged women, the Inamura girl seemed beautiful to him.

· 3 ·

Unaware that she was on display, she went through the ceremony without hesitation, and she herself set the tea before Kikuji.

After drinking, Kikuji looked at the bowl. It was black Oribe, splashed with white on one side, and there decorated, also in black, with crook-shaped bracken shoots.

"You must remember it," said Chikako from across the room.

Kikuji gave an evasive answer and put the bowl down.

"The pattern has the feel of the mountains in it," said Chikako. "One of the best bowls I know for early spring—your father often used it. We're just a little out of season, but then I thought that for Kikuji . . ."

"But what difference does it make that my father owned it for a little while? It's four hundred years old, after all—its history goes back to Momoyama and Rikyū⁴ himself. Tea masters have looked after it and passed it down through the centuries. My father is of very little importance." So Kikuji tried to forget the associations the bowl called up.

It had passed from Ota to his wife, from the wife to Kikuji's father, from Kikuji's father to Chikako; and the two men, Ota and Kikuji's father, were dead, and here were the two women. There was something almost weird about the bowl's career.

Here, again, Ota's widow and daughter, and Chikako, and the Inamura girl, and other young girls too, were holding the old tea bowl in their hands, and bringing it to their lips.

"Might I have tea from the Oribe myself?" asked Mrs. Ota suddenly. "You gave me a different one last time."

Kikuji was startled afresh. Was the woman foolish, or shameless?

He was overcome with pity for the daughter, still sitting with bowed head.

For Mrs. Ota, the Inamura girl once more went through the ceremony. Everyone was watching her. She probably did not know the history of the black Oribe. She went through the practiced motions.

It was a straightforward performance, quite with-

⁴ Sen Rikyū (1521-91), an early tea master.

out personal quirks. Her bearing, from shoulders to knees, suggested breeding and refinement.

The shadow of young leaves fell on the paper-paneled door. One noted a soft reflection from the shoulders and the long sleeves of the gay kimono. The hair seemed luminous.

The light was really too bright for a tea cottage, but it made the girl's youth glow. The tea napkin, as became a young girl, was red, and it impressed one less with its softness than with its freshness, as if the girl's hand were bringing a red flower into bloom.

And one saw a thousand cranes, small and white, start up in flight around her.

Mrs. Ota took the black Oribe in the palm of her hand. "The green tea against the black, like traces of green in early spring." But not even she mentioned that the bowl had belonged to her husband.

Afterward there was a perfunctory inspection of the tea utensils. The girls knew little about them, and were for the most part satisfied with Chikako's explanation.

The water jar and the tea measure had belonged to Kikuji's father. Neither he nor Chikako mentioned the fact.

As Kikuji sat watching the girls leave, Mrs. Ota came toward him.

"I'm afraid I was very rude. I may have annoyed you, but when I saw you it seemed that the old days came before everything."

"Oh?"

"But see what a gentleman you've become." She looked as if she might weep. "Oh, yes. Your mother. I meant to go to the funeral, and then somehow couldn't."

Kikuji looked uncomfortable.

"Your father and then your mother. You must be very lonely."

"Yes, perhaps I am."

"You're not leaving yet?"

"Well, as a matter of fact . . ."

"There are so many things we must talk about, sometime."

"Kikuji." Chikako called from the next room.

Mrs. Ota stood up regretfully. Her daughter had gone out and was waiting in the garden.

The two of them left after nodding their farewell to Kikuji. There was a look of appeal in the girl's eyes.

Chikako, with a maid and two or three favorite pupils, was cleaning the other room.

"And what did Mrs. Ota have to say?"

"Nothing in particular. Nothing at all."

"You must be careful with her. So meek and gentle—she always manages to make it look as if she could do no one the least harm. But you can never tell what she's thinking."

"I suppose she comes to your parties often?" Kikuji asked with a touch of sarcasm. "When did she begin?"

To escape Chikako's poison, he started into the garden.

Chikako followed him. "And did you like her? A nice girl, didn't you think?"

"A very nice girl. And she would have seemed even nicer if I'd met her without the rest of you hovering around, you and Mrs. Ota and Father's ghost."

"Why should that bother you? Mrs. Ota has nothing to do with the Inamura girl."

"It just seemed the wrong thing to do to the girl."

"Why? If it bothered you to have Mrs. Ota here, I apologize, but you must remember that I didn't invite her. And you're to think of the Inamura girl separately."

"I'm afraid I have to go." He stopped. If he went on walking with Chikako, there was no telling when she would leave him.

By himself again, he noted that the azaleas up the side of the mountain were in bud. He heaved a deep sigh.

He was disgusted with himself for having let Chikako's note lure him out; but the impression of the girl with the thousand-crane kerchief was fresh and clean.

It was perhaps because of her that the meeting with two of his father's women had upset him no more than it had.

The two women were still here to talk of his father, and his mother was dead. He felt a surge of something like anger. The ugly birthmark came to him again.

An evening breeze was rustling the new leaves. Kikuji walked slowly, hat in hand.

From a distance he saw Mrs. Ota standing in the shadow of the main gate.

He looked for a way of avoiding her. If he climbed to the right or left, he could probably leave the temple by another exit.

Nevertheless, he walked toward the gate. A suggestion of grimness came over his face.

Mrs. Ota saw him, and came toward him. Her cheeks were flushed.

"I waited for you. I wanted to see you again. I must seem brazen, but I had to say something more. If we had said good-by there, I would have had no way of knowing when I might see you again."

"What happened to your daughter?"

"Fumiko went on ahead. She was with a friend."

"She knew, then, that you would be waiting for me?"

"Yes." She looked into his eyes.

"I doubt if she approves. I felt very sorry for her back there. It was clear that she did not want to see me." The words may have been blunt, and again they may have been circumspect; but her answer was quite straightforward.

"It was a trial for Fumiko to see you."

"Because my father caused her a great deal of pain."

Kikuji meant to suggest that Mrs. Ota had caused him a great deal of pain.

"Not at all. Your father was very good to her. Sometime I must tell you about it. At first she would not be friendly, no matter how kind he was to her; but then, toward the end of the war, when the air raids were bad, she changed. I have no idea why. In her own way, she did her very best for him. Her very best, I say, but she was only a girl. Her best was going out to buy chicken and fish and the like for him. She was very determined, and she didn't mind taking risks. She went out into the country for rice, even during the raids. Your father was astonished, the change was so sudden. I found it very touching myself, so touching that it almost hurt. And at the same time I felt that I was being scolded."

Kikuji wondered if he and his mother might also have had favors from the Ota girl. The remarkable gifts his father brought home from time to time— were they among her purchases?

"I don't know why Fumiko changed so. Maybe it was because we didn't know from one day to the next whether we would still be alive. I suppose she was feeling sorry for me, and she went to work for your father too."

In the confusion of defeat, the girl must have known how desperately her mother clung to Kikuji's father. In the violent reality of those days, she must have left behind the past that was her own father, and seen only the present reality of her mother.

"Did you notice the ring Fumiko was wearing?"

"No."

"Your father gave it to her. Even when he was with me, your father would go home if there was an air-raid warning. Fumiko would see him home, and no one could talk her out of it. There was no telling what would happen if he went alone, she would say. One night she didn't come back. I hoped she had stayed at your house, but I was afraid the two of them had been killed. Then in the morning she came home and said that she had seen him as far as your gate and spent the rest of the night in an air-raid shelter. He thanked her the next time he came, and gave her that ring. I'm sure she was embarrassed to have you see it."

Kikuji was most uncomfortable. And it was odd that the woman seemed to expect sympathy as a matter of course.

His mood was not clearly one of dislike or distrust, however. There was a warmth in her that put him off guard.

When the girl had desperately been doing everything she could for his father, had she been watching her mother, and yet unable to watch?

Kikuji sensed that Mrs. Ota was talking of her own love as she talked of the girl.

She seemed to be pleading something with all the passion she had, and in its final implications the plea did not seem to make a distinction between Kikuji's father and Kikuji himself. There was a deep, affectionate nostalgia in it, as if she meant to be talking to Kikuji's father.

The hostility which Kikuji, with his mother, had felt for Mrs. Ota had lost some of its strength, though it had not entirely disappeared. He even feared that unless he was careful he might find in himself the father loved by Mrs. Ota. He was tempted to imagine that he had known this woman's body long ago.

His father had soon left Chikako, Kikuji knew, but he had stayed with Mrs. Ota until his death. Still it seemed probable that Chikako had treated Mrs. Ota with derision. Kikuji saw signs of much

the same cruelty in himself, and he found something seductive in the thought that he could do her
injury with a light heart.

"Do you often go to Kurimoto's affairs?" he
asked. "Didn't you have enough of her in the old
days?"

"I had a letter from her after your father died.
I missed your father a great deal. I was feeling very
lonely." She spoke with bowed head.

"And does your daughter go too?"

"Fumiko? Fumiko just keeps me company."

They had crossed the tracks and passed the North
Kamakura Station, and were climbing the hill opposite the Engakuji.

· 4 ·

Mrs. Ota was at least forty-five, some twenty
years older than Kikuji, but she had made him forget her age when they made love. He felt that he
had had a woman younger than he in his arms.

Sharing a happiness that came from the woman's
experience, Kikuji felt none of the embarrassed reti-
cence of inexperience.

He felt as if he had for the first time known
woman, and as if for the first time he had known

himself as a man. It was an extraordinary awakening. He had not guessed that a woman could be so wholly pliant and receptive, the receptive one who followed after and at the same time lured him on, the receptive one who engulfed him in her own warm scent.

Kikuji, the bachelor, usually felt soiled after such encounters; but now, when the sense of defilement should have been keenest, he was conscious only of warm repose.

He usually wanted to make his departure roughly; but today it was as though for the first time someone was warmly near him and he was drifting willingly along. He had not until then seen how the wave of woman followed after. Giving his body to the wave, he even felt a satisfaction as of drowsing off in triumph, the conqueror whose feet were being washed by a slave.

And there was a feeling of the maternal about her.

"Kurimoto has a big birthmark. Did you know it?" He bobbed his head as he spoke. Without forethought, he had introduced the unpleasant. Possibly because the fibres of his consciousness had slackened, however, he did not feel that he was wronging Chikako. He put out his hand. "Here, on the breast, like this."

Something had risen inside him to make him say it. Something itchy that wanted to rise against Kikuji himself and injure the woman. Or perhaps it only hid a sweet shyness in wanting to see her body, to see where the mark should be.

"How repulsive!" She quickly brought her kimono together. But there seemed to be something she could not quite accept. "I hadn't known," she said quietly. "You can't see it under the kimono, can you?"

"It's not impossible."

"No! How could you possibly?"

"You could see it if it were here, I should imagine."

"Stop. Are you looking to see if I have a mark too?"

"No. But I wonder how you'd feel at a time like this if you did have a mark."

"Here?" Mrs. Ota looked at her own breast. "But why do you have to speak of it? Does it make any difference?" In spite of the protest, her manner was unresisting. The poison disseminated by Kikuji seemed to have had no effect. It flowed back to Kikuji himself.

"But it does make a difference. I only saw it once, when I was eight or nine years old, and I can see it even now."

"Why?"

"You were under the curse of that birthmark yourself. Didn't Kurimoto come at you as if she were fighting for Mother and me?"

Mrs. Ota nodded, and pulled away. Kikuji put strength into his embrace.

"She was always conscious of that birthmark. It made her more and more spiteful."

"What a frightening idea."

"And maybe too she was out for revenge against my father."

"For what?"

"She thought he was belittling her because of the birthmark. She may even have persuaded herself that he left her because of it."

"Let's not talk about the repulsive thing." But she seemed to be drawing no clear picture of the birthmark in her mind. "I don't suppose Miss Kurimoto worries about it any more. The pain must have gone long ago."

"Does pain go away and leave no trace, then?"

"You sometimes even feel sentimental for it." She spoke as if still half in a dream.

Then Kikuji said what he had meant at all costs not to say.

"You remember the girl on your left this afternoon?"

"Yes, Yukiko. The Inamura girl."

"Kurimoto invited me today so that I could inspect her."

"No!" She gazed at him with wide, unblinking eyes. "It was a *miai*, was it? I never suspected."

"Not a *miai*, really."

"So that was it. On the way home from a *miai*." A tear drew a line from her eye down to the pillow. Her shoulders were quivering. "It was wrong. Wrong. Why didn't you tell me?"

She pressed her face to the pillow.

Kikuji had not expected so violent a response.

"If it's wrong it's wrong, whether I'm on the way home from a *miai* or not." He was being quite honest. "I don't see the relationship between the two."

But the figure of the Inamura girl at the tea hearth came before him. He could see the pink kerchief and the thousand cranes.

The figure of the weeping woman had become ugly.

"Oh, it was wrong. How could I have done it? The things I'm guilty of." Her full shoulders were shaking.

If Kikuji had regretted the encounter, he would have had the usual sense of defilement. Quite aside from the question of the *miai*, she was his father's woman.

But he had until then felt neither regret nor re-vulsion.

He did not understand how it had happened, it had happened so naturally. Perhaps she was apolo-gizing for having seduced him, and yet she had probably not meant to seduce him, nor did Kikuji feel that he had been seduced. There had been no suggestion of resistance, on his part or the woman's. There had been no qualms, he might have said.

They had gone to an inn on the hill opposite the Engakuji, and they had had dinner, because she was still talking of Kikuji's father. Kikuji did not have to listen. Indeed it was in a sense strange that he listened so quietly; but Mrs. Ota, evidently with no thought for the strangeness, seemed to plead her yearning for the past. Listening, Kikuji felt ex-pansively benevolent. A soft affection enveloped him.

It came to him that his father had been happy.

Here, perhaps, was the source of the mistake. The moment for sending her away had passed, and, in the sweet slackening of his heart, Kikuji gave himself up.

But deep in his heart there remained a dark shadow. Venomously, he spoke of Chikako and the Inamura girl.

The venom was only too effective. With regret came defilement and revulsion, and a violent wave of self-loathing swept over him, pressing him to say something even crueller.

"Let's forget about it. It was nothing," she said. "It was nothing at all."

"You were remembering my father?"

"What!" She looked up in surprise. She had been weeping, and her eyelids were red. The eyes were muddied, and in the wide pupils Kikuji still saw the lassitude of woman. "If you say so, I have no answer. But I'm a very unhappy person."

"You needn't lie to me." Kikuji roughly pulled her kimono open. "If there were even a birthmark, you'd never forget. The impression . . ." He was taken aback at his own words.

"You aren't to stare at me. I'm not young any more."

Kikuji came at her as if to bite.

The earlier wave returned, the wave of woman.

He fell asleep in security.

Half awake and half asleep, he heard birds chirping. It was as if he were awakening for the first time to the call of birds.

A morning mist wet the trees at the veranda. Kikuji felt that the recesses of his mind had been washed clean. He thought of nothing.

Mrs. Ota was sleeping with her back to him. He wondered when she had turned away. Raising himself to an elbow, he looked into her face in the semi-darkness.

· 5 ·

Some two weeks later, the Ota girl called on Kikuji.

He had the maid show her into the parlor. In an effort to quiet the beating of his heart, he opened the tea cupboard and took out sweets. Had the girl come alone, or was her mother waiting outside, unable to come in?

The girl stood up as he opened the door. Her head was bowed, and Kikuji saw that the out-thrust lower lip was firmly closed.

"I've kept you waiting." Kikuji opened the glass doors to the garden. As he passed behind the girl, he caught a faint scent from the white peony in the vase. Her full shoulders were thrown slightly forward.

"Please sit down." Kikuji took a seat himself. He was strangely composed, seeing the image of the mother in the daughter.

"I really should have telephoned first." Her head was still bowed.

"Not at all. But I'm surprised that you were able to find the place."

She nodded.

Then Kikuji remembered: during the air raids, she had seen his father as far as the gate. He had heard the story from Mrs. Ota at the Engakuji.

On the point of mentioning it, he stopped himself. He looked at the girl.

Mrs. Ota's warmth came over him like warm water. She had gently surrendered everything, he remembered, and he had felt secure.

Because of that security, he now felt his wariness fade. The girl did not return his gaze.

"I . . ." She broke off and looked up. "I have a request to make. About my mother."

Kikuji caught his breath.

"I want you to forgive her."

"To forgive her?" Kikuji sensed that the mother had told the daughter of him. "I'm the one to be forgiven if anyone is."

"I'd like you to forgive her for your father too."

"And isn't he the one to be forgiven? But my mother is no longer alive in any case, and who would do the forgiving?"

"It is Mother's fault that your father died so soon. And your mother. I told Mother so."

"You are imagining things. You musn't be unkind to her."

"Mother should have died first." She spoke as if she found the shame intolerable.

Kikuji saw that she was speaking of his own relations with her mother. How deeply they must have wounded and shamed her!

"I want you to forgive her," the girl said once more, an urgent plea in her voice.

"It's not a question of forgiving or not forgiving." Kikuji spoke with precision. "I am grateful to your mother."

"She is bad. She is no good, and you must have nothing more to do with her. You are not to worry yourself about her." The words poured out, and her voice was trembling. "Please."

Kikuji understood what she meant by forgive. She included a request that he see no more of Mrs. Ota.

"Don't telephone her." The girl flushed as she spoke. She raised her head and looked at him, as if in an effort to master the shyness. There were tears in the wide, near-black eyes, and there was no trace of malice. The eyes were submitting a desperate petition.

"I understand," said Kikuji. "I'm sorry."

"Please, I beg you." As the shyness deepened, the flush spread to her long, white throat. She was in European dress, and a necklace set off the beauty of the throat. "She made an appointment over the telephone and then didn't keep it. I stopped her. When she tried to go out, I hung on her and wouldn't let her." The voice now carried a note of relief.

Kikuji had telephoned Mrs. Ota the third day after their meeting. She had seemed overjoyed, and yet she had not come to the appointed tea room.

Besides the one telephone call, Kikuji had had no communication with her.

"Afterwards I felt sorry for her, but at the time it was so wretched—I was so desperate to keep her from going. She told me to refuse for her, then, and I got as far as the telephone and couldn't say anything. Mother was staring at the telephone, and tears were streaming over her face. She felt you there in the telephone, I know she did. That is the sort of person she is."

The two were silent for a time. Then Kikuji spoke. "Why did you leave your mother to wait for me after Kurimoto's party?"

"Because I wanted you to know that she was not as bad as you might have thought."

"She is too much the reverse of bad."

The girl looked down. Below the well-shaped nose he could see the small mouth and the lower lip, thrust out as if in a pout. The softly rounded face reminded him of her mother.

"I knew that Mrs. Ota had a daughter, and I used to wish I could talk to the girl about my father."

She nodded. "I used to wish very much the same thing."

Kikuji thought how good it would be to talk freely of his father and take no account of Mrs. Ota.

But it was because he could no longer "take no account" that he was able to forgive her, and at the same time to feel that he was forgiving what she and his father had been. Must he find that fact strange?

Perhaps suspecting that she had stayed too long, the girl hastily stood up.

Kikuji saw her to the gate.

"I hope we will have a chance sometime to talk about my father. And about your mother, and all the beauty there is in her." Kikuji feared that he had chosen a somewhat exaggerated way to express himself. Still, he meant what he had said.

"But you will be getting married soon."

"I will?"

"Yes. Mother said so. It was a *miai* with Inamura Yukiko, she said."

"It was not."

A hill fell away from outside the gate. Halfway down the slope the street curved, and, looking back, one saw only the trees in Kikuji's garden.

The image of the girl with the thousand-crane kerchief came to him. Fumiko stopped and said good-by.

Kikuji started back toward the house.

The Grove in the Evening Sun

CHIKAKO TELEPHONED Kikuji's office.
 "Are you going straight home?"

He would be going home, but he frowned.
'Well . . ."

'You go straight home. For your father's sake.

This is the day he had his tea ceremony every year. I could hardly sit still, thinking about it."

Kikuji said nothing.

"The tea cottage . . . Hello? . . . I was cleaning the tea cottage, and all of a sudden I wanted to do some cooking."

"Where are you calling from?"

"Your house. I'm at your house. I'm sorry—I should have said so."

Kikuji was startled.

"I just couldn't sit still. I thought I'd feel better if you would let me clean the cottage. I should have telephoned first, I know, but you would have been sure to refuse me."

Kikuji had not used the tea cottage since his father's death.

In the months before she died, his mother had gone out to sit in the cottage from time to time. She did not put embers in the hearth, however, but carried hot water with her. Kikuji would wait uneasily for her to come back. It troubled him to imagine what she might be thinking, alone in the stillness.

He had sometimes wanted to look in on her, but to the end he had kept his distance.

Chikako rather than his mother had taken care of the cottage while his father was alive. His mother had but rarely gone into it.

It had been closed since his mother's death. A maid who had been with the family from his father's time would air it several times a year.

"How long has it been since you last cleaned the place? I cannot get rid of the mildew, no matter how hard I rub." Her voice was brassy. "And while I was about the housecleaning, I wanted to do some cooking. The idea just came to me. I don't have everything I need, but I hope you'll come right home."

"You don't think you're being a little forward?"

"You'll be lonely by yourself. Suppose you bring a few friends from the office."

"Very unlikely. Not one of them is interested in tea."

"All the better. They won't expect too much, and the preparations have been very inadequate. We can all relax."

"Not the slightest chance." Kikuji flung the words into the telephone.

"A pity. What shall we do? Do you suppose—someone who shared the hobby with your father? But we couldn't, at this hour. Shall I call the Inamura girl?"

"You're joking."

"Why shouldn't I call her? The Inamuras are very interested in you, and this will be your chance to see the girl again, and have a good look at her and talk to her. I'll just call her up. If she comes it will be a sign that as far as she's concerned everything is settled."

"I don't like anything about the idea." Kikuji's chest tightened painfully. "And 1 won't be coming home anyway."

"This isn't the sort of question you settle over the telephone. We'll talk about it later. Well, that's how things are. Come right home, now."

"How things are—what are you talking about?"

"Oh, don't worry. I'm just being bold." The venomous persistence came at him over the wire.

He thought of the birthmark that covered half her breast. The sound of her broom became the sound of a broom sweeping the contents from his skull, and her cloth polishing the veranda a cloth rubbing at his skull.

Revulsion came first. But it was a remarkable story, this marching into a house with the master out, and taking over the kitchen.

She would have been easier to forgive if she had limited herself to cleaning the cottage and arranging flowers in memory of his father.

Into his revulsion flashed the image of the Inamura girl, a vein of light.

Chikako had drifted away after his father's death.

Did she mean to use the Inamura girl as bait to draw him near again? Was he again to become entangled with her?

As always, she had made herself interesting, however—one smiled ruefully at her, and one's defenses fell. Yet her obstinacy seemed to carry a threat.

Kikuji feared that the threat came from his own weakness. Weak and quivering, he could not really be angry at the importunate woman.

Had she sensed the weakness, and was she hastening to take advantage of it?

Kikuji went to the Ginza, and into a dirty little bar.

Chikako was right: he should go home. But the weakness was an oppressive burden to have to take with him.

Chikako could hardly know that Kikuji had spent the night in that Kamakura inn. Or had she seen Mrs. Ota afterward?

It seemed to him that there was more than Chikako's usual brazenness in this persistence.

Yet perhaps, in the way most natural for her, she was pushing the Inamura girl's suit.

He fidgeted for a time in the bar, then started home.

As the train approached Tokyo Central Station, he looked down upon a tree-lined avenue.

It ran east and west, almost at right angles to the

railroad. The western sun poured into it, and the street glittered like a sheet of metal. The trees, with the sun behind them, were darkened almost to black. The shadows were cool, the branches wide, the leaves thick. Solid Occidental buildings lined the street.

There were strangely few people. The street was quiet and empty all the way to the Palace moat. The dazzlingly bright streetcars too were quiet.

Looking down from the crowded train, he felt that the avenue alone floated in this strange time of evening, that it had been dropped here from some foreign country.

He had the illusion that the Inamura girl was walking in the shade of the trees, the pink kerchief and its thousand white cranes under her arm. He could see the cranes and the kerchief vividly.

He sensed something fresh and clean.

His chest rose—the girl might even now be arriving at his door.

But what had Chikako had in mind, telling him to bring friends, and, when he refused, suggesting that she call the Inamura girl? Had she meant from the start to call the girl? Kikuji did not know.

Chikako came hurrying to the door. "You're alone?"

Kikuji nodded.

"It's better that way. She's here." Chikako took

🌷

his hat and briefcase. "You made a stop on your way home, I see." Kikuji wondered if his breath smelled of liquor. "Where was it? I called the office again and was told you had left, and I knew how much time it would take you to get home."

"I shouldn't be surprised at anything you do, I suppose."

She made no apology for having come uninvited and taken over the house.

She evidently meant to go with him to his room and help him change to the kimono the maid had laid out.

"Don't bother. I can manage by myself." In shirt sleeves, Kikuji withdrew to his room.

But Chikako was still waiting when he came out.

"Aren't bachelors remarkable."

"Very."

"But it's not a good way to live. Let's make a change."

"I learned my lesson from watching my father."

She glanced up at him.

She had borrowed an apron from the maid, and her sleeves were pushed up. The apron had belonged to Kikuji's mother.

The flesh of her arms was disproportionately white and full, and the muscle at the inside of the elbow was like cord. Very strange, thought Kikuji. The flesh seemed hard and heavy.

"I suppose the cottage would be best." Her manner became more businesslike. "I have her in the main house now."

"Is there a light out there? I don't remember having seen one."

"We might eat by candlelight. That would be even more interesting."

"Not for me."

Chikako seemed to remember something. "When I spoke to Miss Inamura over the telephone, she asked if I meant that her mother was to come too. I said it would be still better if we could have the two of them. But there were reasons why the mother couldn't come, and we made it just the girl."

" 'We made it,' you say, but you did it all by yourself. Don't you suppose she thought it just a little rude, being summoned out with no warning?"

"No doubt. But here she is. She's here, and doesn't that cancel out my rudeness?"

"Why should it?"

"Oh, it does. She's here, and that means that as far as she's concerned matters are going beautifully. I can be forgiven if I seem a little odd along the way. When everything is settled, the two of you can have a good laugh over what an odd person Kurimoto is. Talks that are going to be settled are going to be settled, whatever you do in the process. That's been my experience."

Thus Chikako made light of her behavior. It was as if she had read Kikuji's mind.

"You've talked it over with her then?"

"That I have." And don't you be dodging the issue, her manner seemed to say.

Kikuji walked down the veranda toward the parlor. A large pomegranate tree grew half under the eaves. He struggled to control himself—he must not show displeasure when he received the Inamura girl.

As he looked into the deep shadow of the pomegranate, he thought again of Chikako's birthmark. He shook his head. The last of the evening sunlight shone on the garden stones below the parlor.

The doors were open, and the girl was near the veranda.

Her brightness seemed to light the far corners of the large, dusky room.

There were Japanese irises in the alcove.

There were Siberian irises on the girl's obi. Perhaps it was coincidence. But irises were most ordinary flowers for the season, and perhaps she had planned the combination.

The Japanese irises sent their blossoms and leaves high into the air. One knew that Chikako had arranged them a short time before.

. 2 .

The next day, Sunday, was rainy.

In the afternoon, Kikuji went alone to the tea cottage, to put away the utensils they had used.

And he went too in search of the fragrance of the Inamura girl.

He had the maid bring an umbrella, and as he stepped down into the garden he noticed that there was a leak in the rain gutter on the eaves. A stream of water fell just in front of the pomegranate tree.

"We'll have to have that repaired," he said to the maid.

"Yes, sir."

Kikuji remembered that for some time the sound of falling water had bothered him on rainy nights.

"But once we start making repairs, there'll be no end to them. I ought to sell the place before it falls apart."

"People with big houses all seem to be saying that. The young lady yesterday was very surprised at the size of this house. She spoke as if she might live here some day."

The maid was telling him not to sell it.

"Miss Kurimoto mentioned the possibility?"

"Yes, sir. And when the young lady came, Miss

Kurimoto seems to have shown her through the house."

"What will she do next!"

The girl had said nothing to Kikuji of having seen the house.

He thought she had gone only from the sitting room to the tea cottage, and now he wanted to go from the sitting room to the cottage himself.

He had not slept the night before.

He had felt that the scent of the girl would still be in the cottage, and he had wanted to go out in the middle of the night.

"She will always be far away," he had thought, trying to make himself sleep.

He had not suspected that Chikako had marched her through the house.

Ordering the maid to bring charcoal embers, he went out over the stepping stones.

Chikako, who lived in Kamakura, had left with the Inamura girl. The maid had cleaned the cottage.

Kikuji's only duty was to put away the utensils piled in one corner. But he was not sure where they all belonged.

"Kurimoto would know," he muttered to himself, looking at the picture in the alcove. It was a small Sōtatsu[1] wash in light ink, delicately colored.

[1] An early Edo Period painter the dates of whose birth and death are uncertain.

"Who is the poet?" the Inamura girl had asked the evening before, and Kikuji had not been able to answer.

"I wouldn't know, I'm afraid, without a poem. In this sort of portrait, every poet looks exactly like every other poet," he said.

"It will be Muneyuki,"[2] said Chikako. "'Forever green, the pines are yet greener in the spring.' The painting is already a little out of season, but your father was very fond of it. He used to take it out in the spring."

"But from the picture it could be Tsurayuki[3] just as well as Muneyuki," Kikuji objected.

Even today, he could find nothing distinctive about the vague figure.

But there was power, a suggestion of mass and weight, in the few quick lines. Looking at it for a time, he seemed to catch a faint perfume, something clean and clear.

The painting and the irises in the sitting room brought back the Inamura girl.

"I'm sorry to have taken so long. I thought it would be best to let the water boil a little while." The maid came with charcoal and a tea kettle.

Because the cottage was damp, Kikuji had meant

[2] Minamoto Muneyuki, died 939.
[3] Ki no Tsurayuki, died 945.

to warm it. He had not thought of making tea.

The maid, however, had used her imagination.

Kikuji absent-mindedly arranged the charcoal and put on the kettle.

Keeping his father company, he had often been through the tea ceremony. He had never been tempted to take up the hobby himself, however, and his father had never pressed him.

Even with the water boiling, he only pushed the lid open a little and sat staring at it.

There was a smell of mildew. The mats too seemed to be damp.

The deep, subdued color of the walls had brought the figure of the Inamura girl out to even better effect than usual; but today they were only dark.

There had been a certain incongruity, as when someone living in a European house wears a kimono. Kikuji had said to the girl: "It must have upset you, being called out by Kurimoto. And it was Kurimoto's idea to bring us out here."

"Miss Kurimoto says that this is the day of your father's tea ceremony."

"So it would seem. I had forgotten about it myself."

"Do you suppose she's being funny, inviting someone like me on a day like this? I haven't been practicing, I'm afraid."

"But I gather that Kurimoto herself only remembered this morning, and came to clean the cottage. Smell the mildew?" He half swallowed the next words: "If we are to be friends, I can't help thinking we would have done better to have someone besides Kurimoto introduce us. I should apologize to you."

She looked at him suspiciously. "Why? If it hadn't been for Miss Kurimoto, who could have introduced us?"

It was a simple protest, and yet very much to the point.

If it had not been for Chikako, the two would not have met in this world.

Kikuji felt as if a glittering whip had lashed at him.

The girl's way of speaking suggested that his proposal was accepted. So it seemed to Kikuji.

The strangely suspicious look in her eyes therefore came blazing at him.

How did she take it when he dismissed Chikako as "Kurimoto"? Did she know that Chikako had been his father's woman, though for but a short time?

"I have bad memories of Kurimoto." Kikuji's voice was near trembling. "I don't want that woman's destinies to touch mine at any point. It's hard to believe that she introduced us."

Having served the others, Chikako came with a

tray for herself. The conversation broke off.

"I hope you won't mind if I join you." Chikako sat down. Bending slightly forward, as though to recover her breath from having been up and at work, she looked into the girl's face. "It's a little lonely, being an only guest. But I'm sure Kikuji's father is happy too."

Unaffectedly, the girl looked at the floor. "I'm hardly qualified to be in Mr. Mitani's cottage."

Chikako ignored the remark and talked on, as memories came to her, of Kikuji's father and the cottage.

Apparently she thought the marriage already arranged.

"Suppose you visit Miss Inamura's house sometime, Kikuji," she said as the two left. "We'll see about making an appointment." The girl only looked at the floor. She evidently wanted to say something, but the words would not come. A sort of primeval shyness came over her.

The shyness was a surprise to Kikuji. It flowed to him like the warmth of her body.

And yet he felt that he was wrapped in a dark, dirty, suffocating curtain.

Even today he could not throw it off.

The dirtiness was not only in Chikako, who had introduced them. It was in Kikuji too.

He could see his father biting at her birthmark

with dirty teeth. The figure of his father became the figure of Kikuji himself.

The girl did not share his distrust of Chikako. This was not the only reason for his own irresolution, but it seemed to be one reason.

While Kikuji was indicating his dislike for Chikako, he was making it seem that she was forcing the marriage through. She was a woman who could so be used.

Wondering whether the girl had sensed all this, Kikuji again felt the lash of that whip. He saw himself, the figure at which it struck, and he was repelled.

When they had finished dinner, Chikako went to prepare the tea utensils. "So it's our fate, is it, to have Kurimoto managing us," said Kikuji. "You and I do not seem to have the same view of that fate." The remark, however, sounded like an attempt to vindicate himself.

After his father's death, Kikuji had not liked to see his mother go into the cottage alone. His father and his mother and Kikuji himself, he saw now, had had each his own separate thoughts in the cottage.

Rain spattered against the leaves.

With the rain on the leaves came the sound of rain on an umbrella. The maid called through the closed door. He gathered that someone named Ota had come.

"The young lady?"

"No, sir, the mother. She's terribly thin. I wonder if she's been ill."

Kikuji quickly got up. He only stood there, however.

"Where shall I take her?"

"The cottage here will do."

"Yes, sir."

Mrs. Ota did not have an umbrella. Perhaps she had left it in the main house.

He thought that rain had struck her face; but it was tears.

He knew that it was tears from the steady flow over the cheeks.

And he had thought they were raindrops—that was the measure of his heedlessness. "What's the matter?" he almost shouted as he came up to her.

Mrs. Ota knelt on the veranda with both hands on the floor before her.

She sank down softly, facing Kikuji.

Drop by drop the veranda near the lintel was wet. The tears fell steadily, and Kikuji again wondered if they might be raindrops.

Mrs. Ota did not turn her eyes from him. The gaze seemed to keep her from falling. Kikuji too felt that she would be in danger if her eyes were to leave him.

There were hollows and small wrinkles around

the eyes, and dark spots below. The fold of the eyelids was emphasized in a strangely morbid way, and the pleading eyes glowed with tears. He felt an indescribable softness in them.

"I'm sorry. I wanted to see you, and I couldn't stay away," she said quietly.

There was softness in the figure too.

She was so thin that he could hardly have borne to look at her if it had not been for the softness.

Her suffering pierced him through. Although he was the cause of the suffering, he had the illusion that in the softness his own suffering was lightened.

"You'll get wet. Come inside." Kikuji suddenly took her in a deep, almost cruel embrace from back to breast, and pulled her to her feet.

She tried to stand by herself. "Let me go, let me go. See how light I am."

"Very light."

"I'm so light. I've lost weight."

Kikuji was a little surprised at himself, abruptly taking the woman in his arms.

"Won't your daughter be worried?"

"Fumiko?"

"Is she with you?" She had called out as though the girl were near by.

"I didn't tell her I was coming." The words were little sobs. "She won't take her eyes off me. At night she is awake if I make the slightest move. She's been strange herself lately, thanks to me." Mrs. Ota was now kneeling upright. "She asked me why I had only one child. She said I should have had a child by Mr. Mitani. She says such dreadful things."

Kikuji sensed from Mrs. Ota's words how deep the girl's sadness must be.

He could not feel it as the mother's sadness. It was Fumiko's.

The fact that Fumiko had spoken of his father's child pierced him like a spear.

Mrs. Ota was still gazing at him. "Maybe she'll even come after me today. I slipped out while she was away. It's raining, and she thought I wouldn't leave."

"Because of the rain?"

"She seems to think I'm too weak now to go out in the rain."

Kikuji only nodded.

"Fumiko came to see you the other day?"

"I did see her. She said I must forgive you, and I couldn't think of an answer."

"I know how she feels. Why have I come, then? The things I do!"

"But I've felt grateful to you."

"It's good to hear you say that. It's quite enough, just that. But I've been very unhappy. You must forgive me."

"What is there to make you feel guilty? Nothing at all, I should think. Or maybe my father's ghost."

The woman's expression did not change. Kikuji felt as if he had clutched at air.

"Let's forget everything," said Mrs. Ota. "I'm ashamed of myself. Why should I have been so upset at a call from Miss Kurimoto?"

"Kurimoto telephoned you?"

"Yes. This morning. She said that everything was settled between you and Mrs. Inamura's Yukiko. I wonder why she had to tell me."

Her eyes were moist, but she suddenly smiled. It was not the smile of one weeping. It was a simple, artless smile.

"Nothing at all is settled," he answered. "Do you suppose Kurimoto has guessed about us? Have you seen her since?"

"No. But she's a person you have to be careful with, and she may know. I must have sounded strange when she telephoned this morning. I'm no good at pretending. I almost fainted, and I suppose I screamed at her. She could tell, I know she could, even over the telephone. She ordered me not to interfere."

Kikuji frowned. He had nothing to say.

"Not to interfere—why, I've only thought of the harm I've done Yukiko. But since this morning I've been frightened at Miss Kurimoto. I couldn't stay in the house." Her shoulders quivered as if she were possessed. Her mouth was twisted to one side, and some outside force seemed to pull it upward. All the unsightliness of her years came to the surface.

Kikuji stood up and laid a hand on her shoulder.

She clutched at the hand.

"I'm frightened, frightened." She looked around the room and shrank away, and suddenly her strength left her.

"In this cottage?"

Confused, Kikuji wondered what she might mean. "Yes," he answered vaguely.

"It's a very nice cottage."

Did she remember that her dead husband had occasionally had tea here? Or was she remembering Kikuji's father?

"This is the first time you've been in the cottage?" he asked.

"Yes."

"What are you looking at?"

"Nothing. Not at anything."

"The painting there is a Sōtatsu."

She nodded, and her head remained bowed in the act.

"And you've never been in the main house?"

"Never."

"Can that be true, I wonder."

"I was there once. Your father's funeral." Her voice trailed off.

"The water is boiling. Suppose we have tea. You'll feel better afterwards, and as a matter of fact I'd like a bowl myself."

"Is it all right?" She started to get up, and reeled slightly.

Kikuji took tea bowls and other utensils from the boxes in the corner. He remembered that the Inamura girl had used them the evening before, but he took them out all the same.

Mrs. Ota's hand was trembling. The lid clinked against the kettle.

She bent over to take up the bamboo tea-measure, and a tear wet the shoulder of the kettle.

"Your father was good enough to buy this kettle from me."

"Really? I hadn't known."

Kikuji found nothing displeasing in the fact that the kettle had belonged to the woman's husband. And he did not think her words strange, so simply had she said them.

"I can't bring it to you." She had finished making tea. "Come for it."

Kikuji went to the hearth, and drank the tea there.

The woman fell across his lap as if in a faint.

He put his arm around her shoulder. The shoulder quivered, and her breathing grew fainter. In his arms, she was soft as a small child.

· 3 ·

He shook her roughly.

As if to strangle her, he grasped her with both hands between throat and collarbone. The collarbone stood out sharply.

"Can't you see the difference between my father and me?"

"You mustn't say that."

Her eyes were closed, and her voice was soft.

She was not yet ready to return from the other world.

Kikuji had spoken less to her than to his own disquieted heart.

He had been led easily into the other world. He could only think of it as another world, in which there was no distinction between his father and himself. So strong was the sense of the other world that afterward this disquietude came over him.

He could ask himself if she was human. If she was pre-human, or again if she was the last woman in the human race.

He could imagine her in this other world, making no distinction between her dead husband and Kikuji's father and Kikuji.

"You think of my father, don't you, and my father and I become one person?"

"Forgive me. The things I've done. The things I've been guilty of." A tear spilled over from the corner of her eye. "I want to die. It would be so pleasant to die now. You were about to strangle me. Why didn't you?"

"You aren't to joke about it. But I do feel a little like strangling someone."

"Oh? Thank you." She arched her long throat. "It's thin. You should have no trouble."

"Could you die and leave your daughter behind?"

"It makes no difference. I'll wear out and die soon in any case. Take care of Fumiko."

"If she is like you."

Suddenly she opened her eyes.

Kikuji was astonished at his own words. They had been quite involuntary.

How had they sounded to the woman?

"See? See how my heart is beating? It won't be long now." She took Kikuji's hand and held it to her breast.

Perhaps her heart had started in surprise at Kikuji's words.

"How old are you?"

Kikuji did not answer.

"Still in your twenties? It's wrong. I'm very unhappy. I don't understand myself."

Pressing one hand to the floor, she half pushed herself up. Her legs were curled beneath her.

Kikuji sat up.

"I didn't come here to spoil things for you and Yukiko. But it's done."

"I haven't decided to marry her. But the truth is that you've washed my whole past for me—or so it seemed when you said that."

"Really?"

"Kurimoto was my father's woman too, and she's the go-between. All the poison from the old days is concentrated in that woman. My father was lucky to have you for the last."

"You must hurry and marry Yukiko."

"That's a question for me to decide."

She stared vacantly at him. The blood left her cheeks, and she pressed a hand to her forehead.

"The room is spinning around."

She had to go home, she said. Kikuji called a cab and got in with her.

She leaned back in one corner, her eyes closed, a thoroughly helpless figure. The last embers seemed in danger of going out.

Kikuji did not see her into the house. As she left the cab, her cold fingers simply left his.

At two the next morning, there was a telephone call from Fumiko.

"Hello. Mr. Mitani? My mother has just . . ." The voice broke for an instant, then continued firmly. "Has just died."

"What! What happened?"

"Mother is dead. She had a heart attack. She has been taking a great deal of sleeping medicine lately."

Kikuji did not answer.

"I'm afraid I—must ask a favor, Mr. Mitani."

"Yes?"

"If there is a doctor you know well, and if it seems possible, could you bring him here?"

"A doctor? You need a doctor? I'll have to hurry."

Kikuji was astonished that no doctor had yet been called. Then, suddenly, he knew.

Mrs. Ota had killed herself. The girl was asking him to help hide the fact.

"I understand."

"Please."

She had thought carefully before calling him, he knew, and she had therefore been able to state the essentials of her business with something like formal precision.

Kikuji sat by the telephone with his eyes closed.

He saw the evening sun as he had seen it after the night with Mrs. Ota: the evening sun through the train windows, behind the grove of the Hommonji Temple.[4]

The red sun seemed about to flow down over the branches.

The grove stood dark against it.

The sun flowing over the branches sank into his tired eyes, and he closed them.

The white cranes from the Inamura girl's kerchief flew across the evening sun, which was still in his eyes.

[4] In the southern outskirts of Tokyo

F. Komatsu.

Figured Shino[1]

O N THE DAY after the seventh-day memorial
services, Kikuji made his visit.

It would be evening if, following his usual sched-
ule, he stopped by on his way home from the office.
He had therefore meant to leave work a little early,
but the day was over before he was able to collect
himself for the task.

[1] A ware from the Oribe kilns (see page 18).

Fumiko came to the door.

"Oh!"

She knelt in the raised entranceway and looked up at him. Her hands were pressed to the floor, as though to steady her shoulders.

"Thank you for the flowers yesterday."

"Not at all."

"I thought I wouldn't see you."

"Oh? But people do sometimes send flowers ahead, and go themselves later."

"Even so, I didn't expect you."

"I sent them from a florist's very near here."

Fumiko nodded simply. "There was no name, but I knew immediately."

Kikuji remembered how he had stood among the flowers and thought of Mrs. Ota.

He remembered that the smell of the flowers had softened the guilt.

And now, softly, Fumiko was receiving him.

She had on a plain cotton dress. Except for a touch of lipstick on her dry lips, she wore no cosmetics.

"I thought it would be best to stay away yesterday," he said.

Fumiko turned slightly to one side, inviting him in

Perhaps because she was determined not to weep, she limited herself to the most ordinary greetings;

but it seemed that she would weep anyway unless she moved or remained silent.

"I can't tell you how happy I was to have the flowers. But you should have come." She stood up and followed him in.

"I didn't want to upset your relatives," he answered—lightly, he hoped.

"That sort of thing doesn't worry me any more." The words were firm and clear.

In the sitting room, there was a photograph before the urn.

There were only the flowers Kikuji had sent the day before.

He thought this strange. Had Fumiko left only his and taken away all the others? Or had it been a lonely memorial service? He suspected that it had.

"A water jar, I see."

He was looking at the vase in which she had arranged his flowers. It was a water jar for the tea ceremony.

"Yes. I thought it would be right."

"A fine Shino piece." For a ceremonial jar, it was rather small.

He had sent white roses and pale carnations, and they went well with the cylindrical jar.

"Mother sometimes used it for flowers. That's why it wasn't sold."

Kikuji knelt to light incense before the urn. He

folded his hands and closed his eyes.

He was apologizing. But love flowed into the apology, to coddle and mollify the guilt.

Had Mrs. Ota died unable to escape the pursuing guilt? Or, pursued by love, had she found herself unable to control it? Was it love or guilt that had killed her? For a week Kikuji had debated the problem.

Now, as he knelt with closed eyes before the ashes, her image failed to come to him; but the warmth of her touch enfolded him, making him drunk with its smell. A strange fact, but, because of the woman, a fact that seemed in no way unnatural. And although her touch was upon him, the sensation was less tactile than auditory, musical.

Unable to sleep since her death, Kikuji had been taking sedatives with saké. He had been quick to awaken, however, and he had had many dreams.

They had not been nightmares. On awakening, he would be drowsy and sweetly drunk.

That a dead woman could make her embrace felt in one's dreams seemed eerie to Kikuji. He was young, and unprepared for such an experience.

"The things I've done!" She had said it both when she spent the night with him in Kamakura and when she came into the tea cottage. The words had brought on the delicious trembling and the little sobs, and now, as he knelt before her ashes and asked what had made her die, he thought he might grant for the moment that it had been guilt. The admission only brought back her voice, speaking of her guilt.

Kikuji opened his eyes.

Behind him he heard a sob. Fumiko seemed to be fighting back tears—one sob had escaped, but only one.

Kikuji did not move. "When was the picture taken?" he asked.

"Five or six years ago. I had a snapshot enlarged."

"Oh? It was taken at a tea ceremony?"

"How did you know?"

The photograph had been cut at the throat, showing only a little of the kimono and nothing of the shoulders.

"How did you know it was a tea ceremony?"

"It has that feeling. The eyes are lowered, and she seems to be busy at something. You can't see the shoulders, of course, but you can feel a sort of concentration in her manner."

"I wondered if it would do. It was taken a little from the side. But it's a picture Mother was fond of."

"It's a very quiet picture. A very good picture."

"I can see now that it was a mistake, though. She doesn't look at you when you offer incense."

"Oh? That's true, I suppose."

"She's lookng away, and down."

Kikuji thought of the woman making tea the day before she died.

As she measured out the tea, a tear fell on the shoulder of the kettle. He went for the tea bowl— she did not bring it to him. The tear on the kettle had dried by the time he had drunk the tea. She fell across his lap the moment he laid down the bowl.

"Mother weighed more when the picture was taken." She hurried over the next words: "And it would have embarrassed me to have the picture too much like myself."

Kikuji looked around at her.

Her eyes, now on the floor, had been fixed on his back.

He had to leave the urn and photograph, and face her.

How could he apologize?

He saw his escape in the Shino water jar. He knelt before it and looked at it appraisingly, as one looks at tea vessels.

A faint red floated up from the white glaze. Kikuji reached to touch the voluptuous and warmly cool surface.

"Soft, like a dream. Even when you know as little as I do you can appreciate good Shino."

"Like a dream of a woman," he had thought, but he had suppressed the last words.

"Do you like it? Let me give it to you in memory of Mother."

"Oh, no. Please." Kikuji looked up in consternation.

"Do you like it? Mother will be happy too, I know she will. It's not a bad piece, I should imagine."

"It's a splendid piece."

"So Mother said. That's why I put your flowers in it."

Kikuji felt hot tears coming to his eyes. "I'll take it, then, if I may."

"Mother will be happy."

"But it doesn't seem likely that I'll be using it for tea. I'll have to turn it into a flower vase."

"Please do. Mother used it for flowers too."

"I'm afraid I don't mean tea flowers. It seems sad for a tea vessel to be leaving the tea ceremony."

"I'm thinking of giving up tea myself."

Kikuji turned to face her, and stood up as he did so.

There were cushions near the doors to the breakfast room. He pushed one out toward the veranda and sat down.

She had been kneeling deferentially on the bare straw matting.

Only Kikuji moved. Fumiko was left in the middle of the room.

🌷

Her hands, gently folded at her knees, seemed about to tremble. She clutched them tightly together.

"Mr. Mitani, you must forgive Mother." Her head sank to her breast.

Kikuji started up, afraid that in the motion she would fall over. "What are you saying? It is I who must ask to be forgiven. I've been trying to think of the right words. But there's no way to apologize, and I'm ashamed to be here with you."

"We are the ones who should be ashamed." The shame came over her face. "I wish I could just disappear."

The flush spread from the unpowdered cheeks over the white throat; and all the wear and anguish came to the surface.

The faint blood color only made the pallor more striking.

A dull pain ran through his chest. "I thought how you must hate me."

"Hate you? Do you think Mother hated you?"

"No. But wasn't it I who made her die?"

"She died because of herself. That is what I think. I worried over it for a whole week.

"You've been here alone all the time?"

"Yes. But that is the way we were, Mother and I."

"I made her die."

"She died because of herself. If you say it was you who made her die, then it was I even more. If I have to blame anyone, it should be myself. But it only makes her death seem dirty, when we start feeling responsible and having regrets. Regrets and second thoughts only make the burden heavier for the one who has died."

"That may be true. But if I hadn't met her . . ." Kikuji could say no more.

"I think it's enough if the dead person can be forgiven. Maybe Mother died asking to be forgiven. Can you forgive her?" Fumiko stood up.

At Fumiko's words, a curtain in Kikuji's mind seemed to disappear.

Was there also a lightening of the burden for the dead? he wondered.

Worrying oneself over the dead—was it in most cases a mistake, not unlike berating them? The dead did not press moral considerations upon the living.

Kikuji looked again at Mrs. Ota's photograph.

· 2 ·

Fumiko brought in two bowls on a tray.

They were cylindrical, a red Raku and a black Raku.

She set the black before Kikuji. In it was ordinary coarse tea.

Kikuji lifted the bowl and looked at the potter's mark. "Who is it?" he asked bluntly.

"Ryōnyū,[2] I believe."

"And the red?"

"Ryōnyū too."

"They seem to be a pair." Kikuji looked at the red bowl, which lay untouched at her knee.

Though they were ceremonial bowls, they did not seem out of place as ordinary teacups; but a displeasing picture flashed into Kikuji's mind.

Fumiko's father had died and Kikuji's father had lived on; and might not this pair of Raku bowls have served as teacups when Kikuji's father came to see Fumiko's mother? Had they not been used as "man-wife" teacups, the black for Kikuji's father, the red for Fumiko's mother?

If they were by Ryōnyū, one could be a little careless with them. Might they not also have been taken along on trips?

Fumiko, who knew, was perhaps playing a cruel joke on him.

But he saw no malice, indeed no calculation, in her bringing out the two bowls.

---

[2] Raku, a Kyoto ware, was first produced in the sixteenth century. Ryōnyū (1756-1834) was the ninth master of the Raku kiln.

He saw only a girlish sentimentality, which also came to him.

He and Fumiko, haunted by the death of her mother, were unable to hold back this grotesque sentimentality. The pair of Raku bowls deepened the sorrow they had in common.

Fumiko too knew everything: Kikuji's father and her mother, her mother and Kikuji, her mother's death.

And they had shared the crime of hiding the suicide.

Fumiko had evidently wept as she made tea. Her eyes were a little red.

"I'm glad I came today," said Kikuji. "I could take what you said a few minutes ago to mean that between the living and the dead there can be no forgiving and not forgiving; but I may think instead that I've been forgiven by your mother?"

Fumiko nodded. "Otherwise Mother can't be forgiven. Not that she could forgive herself."

"But in a way it's rather terrible that I'm here with you."

"Why?" She looked up at him. "You mean it was wrong of her to die? I was very bitter myself—I thought that no matter how she had been misunderstood, death could not be her answer. Death only cuts off understanding. No one can possibly forgive that."

Kikuji was silent. He wondered if Fumiko too had pushed her way to a final confrontation with the secret of death.

It was strange to be told that death cut off understanding.

The Mrs. Ota whom Kikuji knew now was rather different from the mother Fumiko knew.

Fumiko had no way of knowing her mother as a woman.

To forgive or to be forgiven was for Kikuji a matter of being rocked in that wave, the dreaminess of the woman's body.

It seemed that the dreaminess was here too in the pair of Raku bowls.

Fumiko did not know her mother thus.

It was strange and subtle, the fact that the child should not know the body from which she had come; and, subtly, the body itself had been passed on to the daughter.

From the moment she had greeted him in the doorway, Kikuji had felt something soft and gentle. In Fumiko's round, soft face he saw her mother.

If Mrs. Ota had made her mistake when she saw Kikuji's father in Kikuji, then there was something frightening, a bond like a curse, in the fact that, to Kikuji, Fumiko resembled her mother; but Kikuji, unprotesting, gave himself to the drift.

Looking at the uncared-for little mouth, the

lower lip thrust forward as if in a pout, he felt that there was no fighting the girl.

What could one do to make her resist?

That question would have to be asked about Kikuji himself. "Your mother was too gentle to live," he said. "I was cruel to her, and I suspect that I was hitting at her with my own moral weakness. I'm a coward."

"Mother was wrong. Mother was so wrong. Your father, then you—but I have to think that Mother's real nature was different." She spoke hesitantly, and flushed. The blood color was warmer than before.

Avoiding Kikuji's eyes, she bowed and turned slightly away.

"But from the day after Mother died, she began to seem more beautiful. Is it just in my mind, or is she really more beautiful?"

"The two are the same, I suppose, with the dead."

"Maybe Mother died from not being able to stand her own ugliness."

"That doesn't seem likely."

"It was too much—she couldn't bear it." Tears came to Fumiko's eyes. Perhaps she wanted to speak of her mother's love for Kikuji.

"The dead are our property, in a way. We must take care of them," said Kikuji. "But they all died in such a hurry."

She seemed to understand: he meant her parents and his own.

"You're an orphan now, and so am I." His own words made him aware that if Mrs. Ota had not had this daughter, Fumiko, he would have had darker, more perverse thoughts about her.

"You were very good to my father. Your mother told me so." He had said it, and he hoped it had seemed unaffected.

He saw nothing wrong in talking of the days when his father had come to this house as the lover of Fumiko's mother.

Suddenly, Fumiko make a deep bow.

"Forgive her. Mother was really too sad. After that, I hardly knew from one minute to the next when she might die." Her head was still bowed. Motionless, she began to weep, and the strength left her shoulders.

Because she had not expected visitors, she was barefoot. Her feet were curled beneath her, half hidden by her skirt, and she presented a thoroughly shrunken, helpless figure.

The red Raku bowl was almost against her hair, so long that it fell to the floor matting.

She left the room with both hands pressed to her face.

Moments passed, and she did not come back. "I believe I'll be leaving, then," said Kikuji.

She came to the door with a bundle.

"I'm afraid it will be heavy, but try not to mind too much."

"Oh?"

"The Shino."

He was astonished at her quickness: she had emptied the jar, dried it, found a box for it, and wrapped it in a kerchief.

"I'm to take it already? But it had flowers in it."

"Please do take it."

"If I may, then," said Kikuji. The quickness, he sensed, had come from an excess of grief.

"But I won't come to see how you use it."

"Why not?"

Fumiko did not answer.

"Well, take care of yourself." He started out.

"Thank you. It was good of you to come. And—don't worry about Mother. Hurry and get married."

"I beg your pardon?"

He turned back toward her, but she did not look up.

· 3 ·

Kikuji tried putting white roses and pale carnations in the Shino jar.

He was haunted by the thought that he was falling in love with Mrs. Ota, now that she was dead.

And he felt that the love was made known through the daughter, Fumiko.

On Sunday, he telephoned her.

"You're at home by yourself?"

"Yes. It's a little lonely, of course."

"You shouldn't be alone."

"I suppose not."

"I can almost hear the quiet."

Fumiko laughed softly.

"Suppose we have a friend look in on you."

"But I keep thinking that whoever comes will find out about Mother."

Kikuji could think of no answer. "It must be inconvenient. You have no one to watch the house when you want to go out."

"Oh, I can always lock it."

"Suppose you come and see me, then."

"Thank you. One of these days."

"Have you been well?"

"I've lost weight."

"And are you able to sleep?"

"Hardly at all."

"That will never do."

"I'm thinking of closing the house soon and taking a room in a friend's house."

"Soon—when will that be?"

"As soon as I can sell the house."

"The house?"

"Yes."

"You mean to sell it?"

"Don't you think I should?"

"I wonder. As a matter of fact, I'm thinking of selling my own."

Fumiko did not answer.

"Hello? There's no use talking about these things over the telephone. It's Sunday and I'm at home. Can you come over?"

"Yes."

"I have flowers in the Shino, but if you come I can try putting it to the use it was meant for."

"A tea ceremony?"

"Not a real ceremony. But it's a great waste not to use Shino for tea. You can't bring out the real beauty of a tea piece unless you set it off against its own kind."

"But I look even worse than when you were here. I can't see you."

"There will be no other guests."

"Even so."

"You won't reconsider?"

"Good-by."

"Take care of yourself. Excuse me—there seems to be someone at the door. I'll call again."

It was Kurimoto Chikako.

A grim look came over Kikuji's face. Had she heard?

"It's been so gloomy. Rain, rain. The first good day in such a long time, and I'm taking advantage of it." She was already looking at the Shino. "From now into the summer, I'll have more time from lessons, and I thought I'd like to come and sit in your cottage for a while."

She brought out her offerings, sweets and a folding fan. "I suppose the cottage will be all mildewed again."

"I suppose so."

"Mrs. Ota's Shino? May I look at it?" She spoke casually, and turned to examine the Shino.

As she bent toward it, the heavy-boned shoulders fell back. She seemed to exude venom.

"Did you buy it?"

"It was a present."

"Quite a present. A keepsake?" She raised her head and turned back to him. "Really, shouldn't you have paid for a piece like this? I'm a bit shocked that you took it from the girl."

"I'll give the question some thought."

"Do. You have all sorts of tea pieces that belonged to Mr. Ota, but your father paid for every one of them. Even after he was taking care of Mrs. Ota."

"That's not a matter I want to discuss with you."

"I see, I see," said Chikako airily, and stood up. He heard her talking to the maid, and she emerged in an apron.

"So Mrs. Ota committed suicide." The show of unconcern was no doubt designed to catch him off guard.

"She did not."

"Oh? But I knew immediately. There was always something weird about that woman." She looked at him. "Your father used to say that he would never understand her. To another woman, of course, the problem was a little different, but there was something childish about her, no matter how old she got. Well, she wasn't my sort. Sticky and clinging, somehow."

"May we ask you to stop slandering the dead?"

"Oh, please do. But isn't this particular dead person still trying to ruin your marriage? Your father suffered a great deal at the hands of that woman."

It was Chikako who had suffered, thought Kikuji.

Chikako was his father's plaything for a very short time. She had no cause to indict Mrs. Ota. Still, one could imagine how she had hated the woman who was with his father to the end.

"You're too young to understand such people. For your sake, it was good of her to die. That's the truth."

Kikuji turned aside.

"Were we to stand for it, having her interfere with your marriage plans? She died because she couldn't keep down the devil in her even when she knew she was doing wrong. That's the truth too. And then being the woman she was, she thought she would die and go meet your father."

Kikuji felt cold.

Chikako stepped down into the garden. "I'm going out to the cottage and quiet my nerves."

He sat for a time looking at the flowers.

The white and the pale pink seemed to melt into a mist with the Shino.

The figure of Fumiko, weeping alone in her house, came to him.

Her Mother's Lipstick

BACK IN HIS BEDROOM after brushing his teeth, Kikuji saw that the maid had hung a gourd in the alcove. It contained a single morning glory.

"I'll be getting up today," he said, though he got into bed again. Throwing his head back, he looked up at the flower.

"There was a morning glory in bloom," said the

maid from the next room. "You'll be at home again today, then, sir?"

"One more day. But I'll be getting up." Kikuji had been away from work for several days with a headache and cold. "Where was the morning glory?"

"It had climbed the ginger at the far side of the garden."

It was a plain indigo morning glory, probably wild, and most ordinary. The vine was thin, and the leaves and blossom were small.

But the green and the deep blue were cool, falling over a red-lacquered gourd dark with age.

The maid, who had been with the family from his father's time, was imaginative in her way.

On the gourd was a fading lacquer seal-signature, and on its ancient-looking box the mark of the first owner, Sōtan,[1] which, if authentic, would make it three hundred years old.

Kikuji knew nothing about tea flowers, nor was the maid likely to be well informed. For morning tea, however, it seemed to him that the morning glory was most appropriate.

He gazed at it for a time. In a gourd that had been handed down for three centuries, a flower that would fade in a morning.

[1] Sen Sōtan (1578-1658), a tea master, was the grandson of Sen Rikyū (page 20).

Was it more fitting than all those Occidental flowers in the three-hundred-year-old Shino?

But there was something unsettling in the idea of a cut morning glory.

"You expect it to wither right in front of your eyes," he said to the maid at breakfast.

He remembered that he had meant to put peonies in the Shino.

It had already been past the peony season when Fumiko gave him the jar, but he could have found them if he had hunted.

"I'd even forgotten that we had the gourd. You were clever to think of it."

The maid only nodded.

"You saw my father put morning glories in it?"

"No. But morning glories and gourds are both vines, and I thought . . ."

"Both vines!" Kikuji snorted. The poetry had quite vanished.

His head grew heavy as he read the newspaper, and he lay down in the breakfast room.

"Don't bother to make the bed."

The maid, who had been doing the laundry, came in drying her hands. She would clean his room, she said.

When he went back to bed, there was no morning glory in the alcove.

Nor was there a gourd hanging from the pillar.

"Well." Perhaps she had not wanted him to see the fading flower.

He had snorted at the association of the two vines, and yet his father's way of living seemed to survive in the maid.

The Shino jar stood naked in the middle of the alcove. Fumiko, if she were to see it, would no doubt think this treatment unkind.

Upon receiving it, he had put white roses and pale carnations in it, because she had done the same before her mother's ashes. The roses and carnations were flowers that Kikuji himself had sent for the seventh-day memorial services.

He had stopped and bought flowers at the shop from which, the day before, he had sent flowers to Fumiko.

His heart would rise even at the touch of the jar, and he had put no more flowers in it.

Sometimes he would be drawn to a middle-aged woman in the street. Catching himself, he would frown and mutter: "I'm behaving like a criminal."

He would look again and see that the woman did not resemble Mrs. Ota after all.

There was only that swelling at the hips.

The longing at such moments would almost make him tremble; and yet intoxication and fear would meet, as at the moment of awakening from a crime.

"And what has turned me into a criminal?" The

question should have shaken him loose from whatever it was; but instead of an answer there came only intenser longing.

He felt that he could not be saved unless he fled those moments when the touch of the dead woman's skin came to him warm and naked.

Sometimes too he wondered if moral doubts had not sharpened his senses to the point of morbidness.

He put the Shino in its box and went to bed.

As he looked out over the garden, he heard thunder.

It was distant but strong, and at each clap it was nearer.

Lightning came through the trees in the garden.

But when the rain began, the thunder seemed to withdraw.

It was a violent rain. White spray rose from the earth of the garden.

Kikuji got up and telephoned Fumiko.

"Miss Ota has moved."

"I beg your pardon?" He was startled. "Excuse me, but might I . . ." She must have sold the house. "I wonder if you could tell me where she is living."

"Just a moment, please." It seemed to be a maid.

She came back immediately and gave him the address, which she was evidently reading from a notebook. "In care of Mr. Tozaki." There was a telephone.

Fumiko's voice was bright. "Hello. I'm sorry to have kept you waiting."

"Fumiko? This is Mitani. I called your house."

"I'm sorry." Her voice fell, and it was like her mother's.

"When did you move?"

"I . . ."

"And you didn't tell me."

"I've been staying with a friend for several days now. I sold the house."

"Oh?"

"I didn't know whether I should tell you or not. At first I thought I shouldn't, but lately I've begun to feel guilty."

"You ought to."

"Really? You're kind enough to think so?"

As they talked on, Kikuji felt fresh and new, washed clean. There could be this feeling from a telephone conversation, then?

"The Shino you gave me. When I look at it I want to see you."

"Oh? I have another, a little cylindrical tea bowl. I thought of letting you have that too, but Mother used it as an everyday teacup. It has her lipstick on it."

"Oh?"

"Or so Mother used to say."

"The lipstick was just left there?"

"Not 'just left there.' The Shino was reddish to begin with, but Mother used to say that she couldn't rub lipstick from the rim, no matter how hard she tried. I sometimes look at it now that she is dead, and there does seem to be a sort of flush in one place."

Was this only idle talk?

Kikuji could hardly bear to listen. "We're having a real storm. How is it there?"

"Terrible. I was terrified at the thunder."

"But it should be pleasant afterward. I've been away from work for several days, and I'm at home now. If you have nothing else to do, why not come over?"

"Thank you. I'd been meaning to stop by, but only after I found work. I'm thinking of going to work." Before he could answer, she continued. "I'm so glad you called. I *will* see you. I shouldn't see you again, of course."

Kikuji got out of bed when the shower was over.

He was surprised at the outcome of the telephone conversation.

And it was strange that his guilt in the Ota affair seemed to disappear when he heard the daughter's voice. Did it make him feel that the mother was still living?

He shook his shaving brush among the leaves at the veranda, wetting it with rain water.

The doorbell rang shortly after lunch. It would be Fumiko—but it was Kurimoto Chikako.

"Oh, you."

"Hasn't it gotten warm. I've been neglecting you, and I thought I should look in."

"I haven't been entirely well."

"Your color isn't good." She scowled at him.

It had been foolish, he thought, to associate the sound of wooden clogs wtih Fumiko. Fumiko would be wearing European dress.

"Have you had new teeth made?" he asked. "You look younger."

"I had spare time during the rainy season. They were a little too white at first, but they turn yellow in a hurry. They'll be all right."

He led her into the sitting room, which also served as his bedroom. She looked at the alcove.

"I've always found empty alcoves pleasant," said Kikuji. "No hangings to weigh you down."

"Very pleasant, with all this rain. But maybe a few flowers at least." She turned back to him. "What did you do with Mrs. Ota's Shino?"

Kikuji did not answer.

"Shouldn't you send it back?"

"That I think is up to me."

"I'm afraid not."

"It's hardly your place to be giving orders."

"That's not quite true either." She laughed and showed her white teeth. "I came today to tell you what I think." In a quick gesture, she thrust both hands before her, then spread them as if to brush something away. "If you don't get rid of that witch."

"You sound very threatening."

"But I'm the go-between, and I'm to have my say."

"If you're talking about the Inamura girl, I'm sorry to have to refuse your proposal."

"Now, now. That's very small of you, refusing a girl you like just because you don't like the go-between. The go-between is a bridge. Go ahead, step on the bridge. Your father was quite happy to."

Kikuji did not hide his displeasure.

When Chikako put herself into an argument, she threw her shoulders back. "I'm telling you the truth. I'm different from Mrs. Ota. As things went with your father, I was a very light case. I see no reason to hide the truth—I was unfortunately not his favorite game. Just when it started, it was over." She looked down. "But I have no regrets. He was good enough to use me afterward, when it was convenient for him. Like most men, he found it easier to use a woman he had had an affair with. And so, thanks to him, I developed a good, healthy strain of common sense."

"I see."

"You should make use of my healthy common sense."

Kikuji was almost tempted to feel safe with her. There was something in what she said.

She took a fan from her obi.

"When a person is too much of a man or too much of a woman, the common sense generally isn't there."

"Oh? Common sense goes with neuters, then?"

"Don't be sarcastic. But neuters, as you call them, have no trouble understanding men and women too. Have you thought how remarkable it is that Mrs. Ota was able to die and leave an only daughter? It seems just possible that she had something to fall back on. If she died, mightn't Kikuji look after the daughter?"

"What are you talking about?"

"I thought and thought, and all of a sudden I came up against a suspicion: she died to interfere with your marriage. She didn't just die. There was more to it."

"Your inventions can be monstrous sometimes." But even as he spoke, he had to gasp at the force of the invention.

It came like a flash of lightning.

"You told Mrs. Ota about the Inamura girl, didn't you?"

Kikuji remembered, but feigned ignorance. "It was you, wasn't it, who told her that everything was arranged?"

"I did. I told her not to interfere. It was the night she died."

Kikuji was silent.

"How did you know I telephoned? Did she come weeping to you?"

She had trapped him.

"Of course she did. I can guess from the way she screamed at me over the telephone."

"Then it's very much as if you killed her, isn't it?"

"I suppose that conclusion makes things easier for you. Well, I'm used to being the villain. When your father needed a villain, he found me quite ideal. It's not exactly that I'm returning an old favor, but I'm here to play the villain today."

Kikuji knew that she was giving vent to the old, deep jealousy.

"But we won't worry about what goes on backstage." She looked down her nose. "I don't care in the least if you sit there glowering at the nasty old woman who comes meddling. Before long I'll have gotten rid of the witch and made a good marriage for you."

"I must ask you to stop talking about this good marriage you're making for me."

"Certainly. I don't want to talk about Mrs. Ota any more than you do." Her voice softened. "I don't mean that she was bad. She was only hoping that when she died the daughter would naturally go to you."

"The nonsense begins again."

"But isn't it the truth? Do you really think that while she was alive she didn't once think of marrying the daughter off to you? That's very absent-minded of you. Waking and sleeping, brooding over your father, almost bewitched, I used to think —if you want to call her emotions pure I suppose they were. She was half out of her mind, and she managed to involve the daughter too, and finally she gave her life. Pure she may have been, but to the rest of us it all sounds like some terrible curse, some witch's net she was laying for us."

Kikuji's eyes met hers.

Her small eyes rolled up at him.

Unable to shake them off, Kikuji looked away.

He withdrew into himself and let her talk on. His position had been weak from the start, and that strange remark had shaken him.

Had the dead woman really thought of marrying her daughter to him? Kikuji did not want to linger over the possibility. It was unreal, a product of that venomous jealousy. Of ugly suspicions, clinging to her breast like the ugly birthmark.

He was deeply uneasy.

Had he not hoped for the same thing?

One's heart could indeed move from mother to daughter; but if, still drunk in the embrace of the mother, he had not sensed that he was being passed on to the daughter, had he not in fact been the captive of withcraft?

And had his whole nature not changed after he met Mrs. Ota?

He felt numb.

The maid came in. "Miss Ota said she would stop by again if you were busy."

"She left, then?" Kikuji stood up.

. 2 .

"It was good of you to telephone this morning." Fumiko looked up at him, showing the full curve of her long, white throat.

There was a yellowish shadow in the hollow from throat to breast.

Whether it was a play of light or a sign of weariness, it somehow gave him rest.

"Kurimoto is here."

He was able to speak calmly. He had come out

feeling tense and constrained, but at the sight of Fumiko the tension strangely left him.

She nodded. "I saw Miss Kurimoto's umbrella."

"Oh. That one?"

There was a long-handled gray umbrella by the door.

"Suppose you wait in the cottage. Old Kurimoto will be leaving soon."

He wondered why, knowing that Fumiko was coming, he had not sent Chikako away.

"It doesn't make any difference as far as I'm concerned."

"Come on in, then."

Shown into the drawing room, Fumiko greeted Chikako as if she did not suspect the hostility. She thanked Chikako for her condolences.

Chikako hunched her left shoulder and threw her head back, as when she watched a pupil at tea.

"Your mother was such a gentle person. I always feel when I see someone like her that I'm watching the last flowers fall. This is no world for gentle people."

"Mother wasn't as gentle as all that."

"It must have troubled her to die and leave an only daughter behind."

Fumiko looked at the floor.

The mouth with its pouting lower lip was drawn tight.

"You must be lonely. Suppose you take up tea again."

"But . . ."

"It will give you something to think about."

"But I'm afraid I can't afford such luxuries."

"Come, now." Chikako dismissed the remark with a sweep of her hands, which had been folded on her knees. "As a matter of fact, I'm here to air the cottage. The rains seem to be over." She glanced at Kikuji. "Fumiko is here too. Shall we?"

"I beg your pardon?"

"I thought I might be allowed to use the Shino piece you have in memory of Fumiko's mother."

Fumiko looked up.

"And we can all exchange memories."

"But I'll only weep if I go into the cottage."

"Let's weep. We'll all have a good cry. I won't have my way with the cottage once Kikuji is married. It's full of memories, of course, but then . . ." Chikako laughed shortly, and was sober again. "Once we've arranged everything with Mrs. Inamura's Yukiko, you know."

Fumiko nodded. Her face was expressionless. There were signs of fatigue, however, on the round face that so resembled her mother's.

"You'll only embarrass the Inamuras, talking of plans that aren't definite," said Kikuji.

"I'm speaking of a *possible* engagement. But

❦

you're right. It's the good things that attract the villains. You must pretend you've heard nothing, Fumiko."

"Of course." Fumiko nodded again.

Chikako summoned the maid and went out to clean the cottage.

"Be careful," she called back from the garden. "The leaves are still wet here in the shade."

· 3 ·

"It was raining so hard here that you must have heard it over the telephone."

"Can you hear rain over the telephone? But I wasn't listening. Could you hear the rain in my garden?"

Fumiko looked out toward the shrubbery, from beyond which they could hear Chikako's broom.

Kikuji too looked out. "I didn't think so at the time, but afterward I began to wonder. It was a real cloudburst."

"I was terrified at the thunder."

"So you said over the telephone."

"I'm like my mother in all sorts of trivial ways. When I was little, Mother used to cover my head with her kimono sleeves whenever it thundered.

And when she went out in the summertime, she would look up at the sky and ask if anyone thought it would thunder. Even now, sometimes, I want to cover my head." Shyness seemed to creep in from her shoulders toward her breast. "I brought the Shino bowl." She stood up.

She laid the bowl, still wrapped in a kerchief, at Kikuji's knee.

Kikuji hesitated, however, and Fumiko herself untied it.

"I suppose your mother used the Raku for an everyday cup? It was Ryōnyū?"

"Yes. But Mother didn't think ordinary tea looked right in either red or black Raku. She used this bowl instead."

"You can't see the color against black Raku."

Kikuji made no motion toward taking up the Shino before him.

"I doubt if it's a very good piece."

"I'm sure it's very good indeed." But he still did not reach for it.

It was as Fumiko had described it. The white glaze carried a faint suggestion of red. As one looked at it, the red seemed to float up from deep within the white.

The rim was faintly brown. In one place the brown was deeper.

It was there that one drank?

The rim might have been stained by tea, and it might have been stained by lips.

Kikuji looked at the faint brown, and felt that there was a touch of red in it.

Where her mother's lipstick had sunk in?

There was a red-black in the crackle too.

The color of faded lipstick, the color of a wilted red rose, the color of old, dry blood—Kikuji began to feel queasy.

A nauseating sense of uncleanness and an overpowering fascination came simultaneously.

In black enamel touched with green and an occasional spot of russet, thick leaves of grass encircled the waist of the bowl. Clean and healthy, the leaves were enough to dispel his morbid fancies.

The proportions of the bowl were strong and dignified.

"It's a fine piece." Kikuji at length took it in his hand.

"I don't really know, but Mother liked it."

"There's something very appealing about tea bowls for women."

The woman in Fumiko's mother came to him again, warm and naked.

Why had Fumiko brought this bowl, stained with her mother's lipstick?

Was she naive, was she tactless and unfeeling? Kikuji could not decide.

But something unresisting about her seemed to come over to him.

He turned the cup round and round on his knee. He avoided touching the rim, however.

"Put it away. There will be trouble if old Kurimoto sees it."

"Yes." She put it back in the box and wrapped it up.

She had evidently meant to give it to him, but she had lost her chance to say so. Perhaps she had concluded that he did not like it.

She took the package out to the hall again.

Shoulders thrust forward, Chikako came from the garden. "Would you mind taking out Mrs. Ota's water jar?"

"Couldn't you use one of ours, with Fumiko here and all?"

"I don't understand. Can't you see that I want to use it because she *is* here? We'll have this keepsake with us while we exchange memories of her mother."

"But you hated Mrs. Ota so."

"Not at all. We just weren't meant for each other. And how can you hate a dead person? We weren't meant for each other, and I couldn't under-

stand her. And then in some ways I understood her
too well."

"You've always been fond of understanding people too well."

"They should arrange not to be understood quite
so easily."

Fumiko appeared at the veranda, and sat down
just inside the room.

Hunching her left shoulder, Chikako turned to
face the girl.

"Fumiko, suppose we use your mother's Shino."

"Please do."

Kikuji took the Shino jar from a drawer.

Chikako slipped her fan into her obi, tucked the
box under her arm, and went back to the cottage.

"It was something of a shock to hear that you'd
moved." Kikuji too went toward the veranda. "You
sold the house all by yourself?"

"Yes. But it was very simple. I knew the people
who bought it. They were living in Oiso while they
looked for something permanent, and they offered
to trade houses. Theirs was very small, just right
for me, they said. But I could never live by myself,
no matter how small the house, and if I'm to work
it will be easier to live in a rented room. I decided
to have a friend take me in."

"Have you found work?"

"No. When I'm being honest with myself, I have

to admit that there's nothing I'm qualified to do."
Fumiko smiled. "I'd been meaning to come by, once
I found work. I hated the thought of talking to you
while I was still drifting, no house, no work,
nothing."

At such times you *should* talk to me, Kikuji
wanted to say. He thought of Fumiko by herself. It
was not a lonely figure he saw.

"I'm thinking of selling this house too, but I
put it off and put it off. But wanting to sell, I've
left the eaves untended, and you can see how long
it's been since I had the mats refaced."

"You'll be married here, I suppose," she said unaffectedly. "You can have them done then."

Kikuji looked at her. "Kurimoto's story? Do you
think I could marry now?"

"Because of Mother? Mother has made you suffer
enough. You should think of her as something finished long ago."

· 4 ·

Cleaning the cottage took the practiced Chikako
very little time.

"How do you like the company I've put the
Shino in?" she asked. Kikuji did not know.

108 🌸
🌸

Fumiko too was silent. They both looked at the Shino.

Before Mrs. Ota's ashes it had been a flower vase, and now it was back at its old work, a water jar in a tea ceremony.

A jar that had been Mrs. Ota's was now being used by Chikako. After Mrs. Ota's death, it had passed to her daughter, and from Fumiko it had come to Kikuji.

It had had a strange career. But perhaps the strangeness was natural to tea vessels.

In the three or four hundred years before it became the property of Mrs. Ota, it had passed through the hands of people with what strange careers?

"Beside the iron kettle, the Shino looks even more like a beautiful woman," Kikuji said to Fumiko. "But it's strong enough to hold its own against the iron."

The luster glowed quietly from the white depths.

Kikuji had said over the telephone that when he looked at this Shino he wanted to see Fumiko. In the white skin of her mother, had he sensed the depths of woman?

It was a warm day. Kikuji slid open the doors of the cottage.

The maples were green in the window behind

Fumiko. The shadow of the maple leaves, layer upon layer, fell on Fumiko's hair.

Her head and her long throat were in the light of the window, and her arms, below the short sleeves of a dress she was apparently wearing for the first time, were white with a touch of green. Although she was not plump, there was a round fullness in the shoulders, and a roundness too in the arms.

Chikako was gazing at the jar. "You can't bring a water jar to life unless you use it for tea. It's a great waste, cramming foreign flowers in it."

"Mother used it for flowers too," said Fumiko.

"It's like a dream, sitting here with this souvenir of your mother. I'm sure she is as happy to see it here as we are." Was she being sarcastic?

Fumiko, however, seemed not to notice. "I gather that Mr. Mitani means to use it as a flower vase, and I've given up tea myself."

"Oh, you musn't say that." Chikako looked around the cottage. "I do feel most at peace when I'm allowed to sit here. I go to all sorts of tea cottages, of course." She looked at Kikuji. "Next year will be the fifth anniversary of your father's death. We must have a tea ceremony."

"I suppose so. It would be fun to invite all sorts of connoisseurs and use imitation pieces from beginning to end."

"Oh, come. There isn't an imitation piece in your father's whole collection.

"Oh? But don't you think that would be fun?" he asked Fumiko. "This cottage always smells of some mouldy poison, and a really false ceremony might drive the poison away. Have it in memory of Father, and make it my farewell to tea. Of course I severed relations with tea long ago."

"What you're saying is that a meddlesome old woman comes to air the place?" Chikako was stirring tea with a bamboo whisk.

"Perhaps I am."

"You musn't. But then I suppose it's all right to sever old relations when you've struck up new." She brought him tea like a waitress filling an order.

"Listen to his jokes, Fumiko. You must wonder whether this souvenir of your mother hasn't come to the wrong place. I almost feel that I can see your mother's face in it."

Kikuji drank and put the bowl down, and glanced at the Shino.

Perhaps Fumiko could see Chikako's figure reflected in the black lacquer lid.

But Fumiko only sat there absently.

Kikuji did not know whether she was resisting Chikako or ignoring her.

It seemed odd that she could be here in the cottage with Chikako and show no resentment.

She had remained impassive when Chikako spoke of Kikuji's marriage.

From long hostility toward Fumiko and her mother, Chikako made every remark an insult.

Was Fumiko's sorrow so deep that the insults flowed over the surface?

Had her mother's death driven her beyond them?

Or had she inherited her mother's nature, was there in her, too, a strange childishness that left her unable to resist, whether the challenge came from herself or another?

Kikuji did not seem disposed to guard her from Chikako's venom.

He noted the fact, and thought himself odd.

And Chikako, now serving herself, struck him as an odd figure too.

She took a watch from her obi. "These little watches are no good when you're far-sighted. Suppose you give me your father's pocket watch."

"He had no pocket watch."

"Oh, but he did. He often had one with him. When he went to Fumiko's house too, I'm sure." Chikako goggled at her own watch.

Fumiko looked down.

"Ten past two, is it? The hands are running together in one big blur." Her manner became brisk and businesslike. "Miss Inamura has been kind enough to organize a tea group, and they practice at three. I thought I'd just stop by for your answer before I went."

"Tell her very clearly that I'll have to refuse."

"I see. I'm to tell her very clearly." Chikako met the crisis with a laugh. "I must have the group practice in this cottage sometime."

"Maybe we could have Miss Inamura buy the house. I'll be selling it anyway."

Chikako ignored him, and turned instead to Fumiko. "Fumiko, suppose we go at least part of the way together."

"Yes."

"I'll be just a minute putting things away."

"Let me help you."

"You'll help me, will you?" But Chikako hurried into the pantry without waiting for her.

There was a sound of water.

"You still have time," said Kikuji in a low voice. "Don't go off with her."

Fumiko shook her head. "I'm afraid."

"There's nothing to be afraid of."

"I'm afraid."

"Suppose you go out, then, and come back when you've gotten rid of her."

But Fumiko again shook her head. She smoothed the back of her summer dress, wrinkled from kneeling.

Kikuji, still kneeling, was about to put out his hand.

He thought she was going to fall. She flushed crimson.

She had reddened sightly at the mention of the pocket watch, and now all the shame seemed to blaze forth.

She took the Shino water jar into the pantry.

"So you brought your mother's Shino, did you?" came Chikako's husky voice.

Double Star

KURIMOTO CHIKAKO came by to tell Kikuji that Fumiko and the Inamura girl were both married.

With daylight-saving time, the sky was still bright at eight-thirty. Kikuji lay on the veranda after dinner, watching the caged fireflies the maid had bought. Their white light took on a yellow tinge as evening became night. He did not get up to turn on the light, however.

He had been vacationing for some days at a friend's villa on Lake Nojiri, and he had come back that afternoon.

The friend was married and had a baby. Not used to babies, Kikuji did not know whether it was large for its age, or indeed how old it was.

"A well-developed baby," he finally said.

"Not really," the wife answered. "It was tiny when it was born. Now, of course, it's beginning to catch up."

Kikuji passed a hand before the baby's face. "It doesn't blink."

"It can see, but blinking comes a little later."

He had thought it would be perhaps six months old, but in fact it was barely a hundred days old. He understood why the hair of the young wife seemed thin, why her color was bad—she was still recovering from childbirth.

The life of the couple centered upon the baby. They seemed to have time only for the baby, and Kikuji felt a little left out. But on the train back, the thin figure of the wife, worn and somehow drained of life, absently holding the baby in her arms—a quiet, docile young woman, one knew immediately—the figure was with him and would not leave. The friend lived with his family, and perhaps the wife, thus alone with her husband at a lakeside villa after the birth of this first child, felt a security that gave her a dreamy respite from thought.

At home now, lying on the veranda, Kikuji remembered the wife with a poignant, almost reverent affection.

Chikako came upon him there.

She marched into the room. "Well. In pitch dark."

She knelt on the veranda, at Kikuji's feet. "It's hard being a bachelor. You have to lie in the dark, and no one will turn on the light for you."

Kikuji curled his legs. He lay thus for a time, and sat up in distaste.

"No, please. Stay as you are." She held out her right hand as if to motion him down, then made her formal bow. She had been to Kyoto and she had stopped at Hakone on the way back. In Kyoto, at the house of her tea master, she had met one Oizumi, a dealer in tea wares. "We talked and talked about your father. Really, it was the first good talk in such a long time. Oizumi said he'd show me the inn your father used for secret meetings, and off we went to a little inn on Kiya-machi. I suppose your father stayed there with Mrs. Ota. And what did Oizumi do but suggest that I stay there myself? Very insensitive of him. With your father and Mrs.

Ota both dead, even someone like me would feel a little strange there in the middle of the night."

Kikuji said nothing. Chikako was hardly demonstrating her own sensitiveness, he thought.

"You've been to Lake Nojiri?" She already knew the answer. It was her style to examine the maid the moment she arrived, and to come in unannounced.

"I got back just a few minutes ago," Kikuji answered sullenly.

"I've been back several days." Chikako's answer too was curt. Abruptly, she hunched her left shoulder. "And I found when I got back that something very unfortunate had happened. I was shocked. A terrible thing—I don't know how to face you."

She told him that the Inamura girl was married.

In the darkness, Kikuji did not have to hide his surprise.

He was able to answer coolly. "Oh? When?"

"Says he, just as if it didn't concern him."

"But I gave you my refusal more than once."

"At least on the surface you did. So you wanted it to seem. You weren't interested, you wanted it to seem, and a meddlesome old woman came bustling in, and pushed and pushed. Very annoying. But the girl herself was all right."

"What are you talking about?" Kikuji laughed sardonically.

"I imagine you liked the young lady well enough."

"A very nice young lady."

"I saw it all."

"The fact that I think she's a nice girl doesn't mean that I want to marry her."

Yet he had felt a stabbing at the heart, and, as if with a violent thirst, he struggled to draw the girl's face in his mind.

He had met her only twice.

To put her on display, Chikako had had her make tea in the Engakuji Temple. Her performance had been simple and elegant, and the impression was still vivid of the shoulders and the long kimono sleeves, and the hair too, radiant in light through paper doors. The shadows of leaves on the paper, the bright red tea napkin, the pink crape handkerchief under her arm as she walked through the temple grounds to the tea cottage, the thousand white cranes—all of these floated freshly into his mind.

The second time, she had come here, and Chikako had made tea. Kikuji had felt the next day that the girl's perfume lingered on, and even now he could see her obi with its Siberian irises; but her face eluded him.

He could not call up the faces of his own mother and father, who had died three or four years before. He would look at a picture, and there they would be. Perhaps people were progressively harder to paint in the mind as they were near one, loved by one. Perhaps clear memories came easily in proportion as they were ugly.

Yukiko's eyes and cheeks were abstract memories, like impressions of light; and the memory of that birthmark on Chikako's breast was concrete as a toad.

Although the veranda was now dark, Kikuji could see that Chikako was wearing a white crape singlet under her kimono. Even if it had been daylight he could not have seen through to the birthmark; but it was there before him, all the more distinct for the darkness.

"Well, most men wouldn't let a girl get away while they were thinking what a nice girl she was. After all, there's only one Yukiko in this world. You won't find her again if you spend your whole life looking. It's the simple things you don't understand." Her manner was openly scolding. "You're inexperienced and you pamper yourself. Well, this has changed her life and it's changed yours. She was very interested. We can't really say, can we, that you're not responsible if her marriage isn't happy?"

Kikuji did not answer.

"You took a good look at her, I suppose. It doesn't bother you to think that years and years from now a girl like her will remember you and think how much better it would have been if she could have married you?"

There was poison in her voice.

But if the girl was already married, why was all this necessary?

"Fireflies? At this time of the year?" She thrust her head forward. "It's almost fall. There are still fireflies, are there? Like ghosts."

"The maid bought them."

"That's the sort of thing maids do. If you were studying tea, now, you wouldn't put up with it. You may not know, but in Japan we are very conscious of the seasons."

There was indeed something ghostly about the fireflies. Kikuji remembered that autumn insects had been humming on the shores of Lake Nojiri. Very strange fireflies, alive even now.

"If you had a wife, she wouldn't depress you with end-of-the-season things." Suddenly her tone was soft and intimate. "I thought of arranging your marriage as a service to your father."

"A service?"

"Yes. And what else happens while you lie in the dark staring at fireflies? The Ota girl gets married too."

"When?" Kikuji was even more startled.

His show of composure struck him as remarkable,

but something in his voice must have given him away.

"I was just as shocked as you are, coming back from Kyoto and hearing about it. Both of them running off and getting married, as if they'd talked it over beforehand—young people don't give much notice, do they? There I was, feeling pleased that Fumiko had kindly removed herself, and wasn't the Inamura girl married too? And the way she did it. She might as well have slapped me in the face. Well, it's all because of your indecisiveness."

Kikuji had trouble believing that Fumiko was married.

"Did Mrs. Ota succeed in ruining your marriage after all, even if she had to die to do it? But maybe the witch will leave us, now that Fumiko is married." Chikako looked out toward the garden. "Suppose you settle down, and give the trees a good pruning. Even in the dark I can see how you've let them grow. The gloomiest garden I've ever been in."

Kikuji had not called a gardener in the four years since his father's death. He had indeed let the garden grow. There was a dank smell from it that brought back the full heat of the day.

"And I suppose the maid does nothing about sprinkling. You might mention that, at least."

"I'm not sure it's your business."

But though he scowled fiercely at each remark, he let her talk on. So it was whenever he saw her.

Even while she was annoying him, she was seeking to ingratiate herself, and probing. He was used to the trick. He showed his displeasure openly, and he was on guard. Chikako knew all this and for the most part feigned ignorance. Occasionally she let him see how much she did know.

Even while she was annoying him, she rarely said things that startled by their incongruity. Everything went with the self-loathing that had become a part of Kikuji's nature.

Tonight she was probing to see how he had reacted to her news. He was on guard—what could be her reason? She had sought to marry him to Yukiko and to drive Fumiko away; and, although it was hardly her place to wonder how he might feel now, she went on digging into the shadows.

He thought of turning on the lights in the room and at the veranda. It was strange to be here in the dark with Chikako. They were hardly that intimate. She gave him advice about the garden, and he dismissed it as the sort of thing she did. Yet it seemed a nuisance to get up and turn on the lights.

And Chikako, though she had spoken of the darkness the moment she came in, made no motion toward getting up. It was her habit, and indeed her art, to be of service; but Kikuji could see that her ardor in serving him had dimmed. Perhaps she was getting old. Perhaps, again, she had her dignity as a mistress of tea.

"I'm just passing on a message from Oizumi in Kyoto," she said nonchalantly, "but if you ever decide to sell your father's collection he'd like to manage the sale. If you mean to pull yourself together and start a new life now that Yukiko has run away, I don't suppose you'll be in a mood for tea. It makes me a little sad to give up work I had when your father was alive, but I suppose the tea cottage gets only the airings I give it."

Well, well—Kikuji saw everything.

Her aims were only too clear. Having failed to arrange the marriage with Yukiko, she would see no more of Kikuji, and, as her farewell, she would form a partnership with Oizumi to take over the collection. She had discussed the terms in Kyoto.

Kikuji felt less angry than relieved.

"I'm thinking of selling the house too. I may well call on you one of these days."

"We can feel safe with someone who's been in and out of the house since your father's time."

Kikuji suspected that she knew better than he what was in the collection. Possibly she had already calculated the profits.

He looked out toward the cottage. In front of it

there was a large oleander, heavy with blossoms, a vague white blur. For the rest, the night was so dark that he had trouble following the line between trees and sky.

. 2 .

About to leave his office one evening, Kikuji was called back to the telephone.

"This is Fumiko." He heard a very small voice.

"Hello."

"This is Fumiko."

"Oh yes, I recognized you."

"I ought to see you in person, but there's something I must apologize for. If I don't telephone it will be too late."

"I beg your pardon?"

"I mailed a letter yesterday, and I seem to have forgotten the stamp."

"Oh? It hasn't come yet."

"I bought ten stamps when I mailed it, and I still had ten when I got home. I must have been thinking of something else. I wanted to apologize before you got the letter."

"Is that all? Really, you shouldn't worry." Kikuji wondered if the letter was to tell of her marriage. "It calls for congratulations?"

"I beg your pardon? We've always talked over

the telephone and this is the first time I've written. I must have forgotten the stamp while I was wondering whether to mail it."

"Where are you calling from?"

"A public telephone. Tokyo Central Station. Someone is waiting for the booth."

"A public telephone?" Kikuji was not quite satisfied. "Congratulations."

"What? Thank you. I did finally—but how did you know?"

"Kurimoto told me."

"Miss Kurimoto? How could she know? What a frightening person."

"I don't suppose you see Kurimoto any more. The last time—remember?—I heard rain over the telephone."

"So you said. I had just moved, and I was wondering whether to tell you. This time it's the same."

"You should have told me. Ever since I had it from Kurimoto I've been wondering whether I should congratulate you."

"And I just disappeared? It's a little sad, isn't it? One of the missing." Her voice, trailing off, was like her mother's.

Kikuji fell silent.

"But I have to be one of the missing." There was a pause. "It's a dirty little room. I found it when I found work."

"I beg your pardon?"

"It wasn't easy, beginning work in the hottest part of the year."

"I'd imagine not. And newly married too."

"Married? Did you say married?"

"Congratulations."

"Me? Married?"

"You *are* married, aren't you?"

"Me?"

"Didn't you get married?"

"No, no! Could I possibly? With mother just dead?"

"I see."

"Miss Kurimoto said I was married?"

"She did."

"Why? Why did she say it? And did you believe it?" The question seemed to be directed half at Fumiko herself.

"It's no good over the telephone." Kikuji spoke with decision. "Can't I see you?"

"Yes."

"I'll go to Tokyo Central. Wait for me there."

"But . . ."

"Is there somewhere you'd rather meet?"

"I don't like meeting people in strange places. I'll go to your house."

"Shall we go together?"

"That would mean meeting somewhere."

"Can't you come here?"

"No. I'll go to your house by myself."

"Oh? Well, I'm leaving now. If you get there first go on inside."

Taking a train from Tokyo Central, she would be there ahead of him. He wondered, however, if they might not be on the same train. He looked for her in the crowd.

She had indeed reached his house ahead of him.

She was in the garden, said the maid. Kikuji went around the house and saw her sitting on a rock in the shade of the white oleander.

Since Chikako's visit some days before, the maid had been careful to sprinkle the shrubbery before Kikuji came home. She used an old faucet in the garden. The rock seemed damp at Fumiko's sleeve.

When a red oleander floods into bloom, the red against the thick green leaves is like the blaze of the summer sky; but when the blossoms are white, the effect is richly cool. The white clusters swayed gently, and enveloped Fumiko. She was wearing a white cotton dress trimmed at the pockets and the turned-down collar with narrow bands of deep blue.

The light of the western sun fell on Kikuji from over the oleander.

"It's good to see you." There was nostalgia in his voice as he came up to her.

She had been about to speak. "Over the telephone, a few minutes ago . . ." She seemed to shrink away from him as she stood up. Perhaps she had felt that unless she stopped him he would take her hand. "You said that, and I've come to deny it."

"That you're married? I was very surprised."

"Surprised that I was or that I wasn't?" She looked at the ground.

"Well, both. When I heard that you were married, and again when I heard that you weren't."

"Both times?"

"Shouldn't I have been?" Kikuji walked on over the stepping stones. "Suppose we go in from here. You could just as well have waited inside, you know." He sat on the veranda. "I'd come back from a trip and I was lying here, and in marched Kurimoto. It was at night."

The maid called Kikuji into the house, probably to confirm the dinner instructions he had telephoned from the office. While he was inside he changed to a white linen kimono.

Fumiko seemed to have repowdered her face. She waited for him to sit down again.

"What exactly did Miss Kurimoto say?"

"Just that you were married."

"Did you believe it?"

"Well, it was the sort of lie I could hardly believe anyone would tell."

"You didn't even doubt it?" The near-black eyes were moist. "Could I get married now, possibly? Do you think I could? Mother and I suffered together, and with the suffering still here . . ." It was as if the mother were still alive. "Mother and I both presume a great deal on people, but we expect them to understand us. Is that impossible? Are we seeing our reflections in our own hearts?" Her voice wavered on the edge of tears.

Kikuji was silent for a time. "Not long ago I said the same thing. I asked if you thought I could possibly marry. The day of the storm, was it?"

"The day of the thunder?"

"And now you say it to me."

"But it's different."

"You said several times that I would be getting married."

"But your case is so different." She gazed at him with tear-filled eyes. "You're different from me."

"How?"

"Your position, your place."

"My position?"

"Your position is different. Shouldn't I say position? I'll say the degree of darkness, then."

"In a word, the guilt? But mine is deeper."

"No." She shook her head violently, and a tear spilled over, drawing a strange line from the corner of her left eye to her ear. "The guilt was Mother's and she died—if we have to talk about guilt. But I don't think it was guilt. Only sorrow."

Kikuji sat with bowed head.

"If it was guilt," she continued, "it may never go away. But sorrow will."

"When you talk about darkness, aren't you making your mother's death darker than you need to?"

"I should have said the degree of sorrow."

"The degree of sorrow."

"Is the degree of love," he wanted to add; but he stopped himself.

"And there is the question of you and Yukiko. That makes you different from me." She spoke as if she meant to bring the conversation back to reality. "Miss Kurimoto thought Mother was trying to interfere, and she thought I stood in the way too. And so she said I was married. I can't think of any other explanation."

"But she said that the Inamura girl was married too."

For a moment her face seemed to collapse. Again she shook her head violently. "A lie, a lie. That's a lie too. When?"

"When did she get married? Very recently, I suppose."

"It's sure to be a lie."

"When I heard that the two of you were married, I thought it might be true about you," he said in a low voice. "But the other may really be true."

"It's a lie. No one gets married in this heat. In a summer kimono, sweat pouring off—can you imagine it?"

"There's no such thing as a summer wedding?"

"Only now and then. People put weddings off to fall, or . . ." For some reason, tears came to her eyes again, and fell to her knee. She gazed at the wet spot. "But why should Miss Kurimoto tell such lies?"

"She cleverly took me in, did she?" Kikuji deliberated for a time.

But what had brought the tears?

It was certain that at least the report about Fumiko was a lie.

Had Chikako said that Fumiko was married to drive her off, the Inamura girl in fact being married? He weighed the possibility.

There was something in it he could not accept, however. He, too, began to feel that she had lied.

"Well, as long as we don't know whether it's a lie or the truth, we don't know the extent of Kurimoto's prankishness."

"Prankishness?"

"Suppose we call it that."

"But if I hadn't telephoned today I'd have been left married. A fine prank."

The maid called Kikuji again.

He came back with a letter in his hand.

"Your letter, and no stamp." He lightly turned it over.

"No, no. You're not to look at it." She brought herself toward him, still kneeling, and tried to take it from his hand. "Give it back to me."

Kikuji whipped his hands behind him.

Her left hand fell on his knee, and her right hand reached for the letter. With left hand and right hand thus making contradictory motions, she lost her balance. The left hand was behind her to keep her from falling against Kikuji, the right was clutching at the letter, now behind Kikuji's back. Twisting to the right, she was about to fall. The side of her face would be against his chest—but she turned supplely away. The touch of her left hand on his knee was unbelievably light. He could not see how she had supported the upper part of her body, twisted as it was and about to fall.

He had stiffened abruptly as she threw herself upon him; and now he wanted to cry out at the astonishing suppleness. He was intensely conscious of the woman. He was conscious of Fumiko's mother, Mrs. Ota.

At what instant had she recovered and pulled away? Where had the force spent itself? It was a suppleness that could not be. It was like the deepest instinct of woman. Just as he was expecting her to come down heavily upon him, she was near him, a warm odor. That was all.

The odor was strong. It came richly, the odor of a woman who had been at work through the summer day. He felt the odor of Fumiko, and of her mother. The smell of Mrs. Ota's embrace.

"Give it back to me." Kikuji did not resist. "I'm going to tear it up."

She turned away and tore her letter to small bits. The neck and the bare arms were damp with perspiration.

She had suddenly paled as she fell toward him and recovered herself. Then, kneeling again, she had flushed· and in that time, it seemed, the perspiration had come out.

· 3 ·

Dinner, from a near-by caterer, was uninteresting, exactly what one would have expected.

Kikuji's teacup was the cylindrical Shino bowl. The maid brought it to him as usual.

He noticed, and Fumiko's eyes too were on it. "You have been using that bowl?"

"I have."

"You shouldn't." He sensed that she was not as uncomfortable as he. "I was sorry afterward that

I'd given it to you. I mentioned it in my letter."

"What did you say?"

"What . . . Well, I apologized for having given you a bad piece of Shino."

"It's not a bad piece at all."

"It can't be good Shino. Mother used it as an ordinary teacup."

"I don't really know, but I'd imagine that it's very good Shino." He took the bowl in his hand and gazed at it.

"There is much better Shino. The bowl reminds you of another, and the other is better."

"There don't seem to be any small Shino pieces in my father's collection."

"Even if you don't have them here, you see them. Other bowls come into your mind when you're drinking from this, and you think how much better they are. It makes me very sad, and Mother too."

Kikuji breathed deeply. "But I'm moving farther and farther from tea. I have no occasion to see tea bowls."

"You don't know when you might see one. You must have seen much finer pieces."

"You're saying that a person can give only the very finest?"

"Yes." Fumiko looked straight at him, affirmation in her eyes. "That is what I think. I asked you in my letter to break it and throw away the pieces."

"To break it? To break this?" Kikuji sought to divert the attack that bore down upon him. "It's from the old Shino kiln, and it must be three or four hundred years old. At first it was probably an ordinary table piece, but a long time has gone by since it became a tea bowl. People watched over it and passed it on—some of them may even have taken it on long trips with them. I can't break it just because you tell me to."

On the rim of the bowl, she had said, there was a stain from her mother's lipstick. Her mother had apparently told her that once the lipstick was there it would not go away, however hard she rubbed, and indeed since Kikuji had had the bowl he had washed without success at that especially dark spot on the rim. It was a light brown, far from the color of lipstick; and yet there was a faint touch of red in it, not impossible to take for old, faded lipstick. It may have been the red of the Shino itself; or, since the forward side of the bowl had become fixed with use, a stain may have been left from the lips of owners before Mrs. Ota. Mrs. Ota, however, had probably used it most. It had been her everyday tea-cup.

Had Mrs. Ota herself first thought of so using it? Or had Kikuji's father? Kikuji wondered.

There had also been his suspicion that Mrs. Ota, with his father, had used the two cylindrical Raku bowls, the red and the black, as everyday "man-wife" teacups.

His father had had her make the Shino water jar a flower vase, then—he had had her put roses and carnations in it? And he had had her use the little Shino bowl as a teacup? Had he at such times thought her beautiful?

Now that the two of them were dead, the water jar and the bowl had come to Kikuji. And Fumiko had come too.

"I'm not just being childish. I really do wish you would break it. You liked the water jar I gave you, and I remembered the other Shino and thought it would go with the jar. But afterward I was ashamed."

"I shouldn't be using it as a teacup. It's much too good."

"But there are so many better pieces. You'll drink from this and think of them. I'll be very unhappy."

"But do you really believe that you can't give away anything except the finest pieces?"

"It depends on the person and the circumstances."

The words had rich overtones.

Was Fumiko kind enough to think that for a souvenir of her mother, a souvenir of Fumiko herself —perhaps something more intimate than a souvenir —only the finest would do?

The desire, the plea, that only the finest be left

to recall her mother came across to Kikuji. It came as the finest of emotions, and the water jar was its witness.

The very face of the Shino, glowing warmly cool, made him think of Mrs. Ota. Possibly because the piece was so fine, the memory was without the darkness and ugliness of guilt.

As he looked at the masterpiece it was, he felt all the more strongly the masterpiece Mrs. Ota had been. In a masterpiece there is nothing unclean.

He looked at the jar and he wanted to see Fumiko, he had said over the telephone that stormy day. He had been able to say it only because the telephone stood between. Fumiko had answered that she had another Shino piece, and brought him the bowl.

It was probably true that the bowl was weaker than the jar.

"I seem to remember that my father had a portable tea chest. He used to take it with him when he went traveling," mused Kikuji. "The bowl he kept in it must be much worse than this."

"What sort of bowl is it?"

"I've never seen it myself."

"Show it to me. It's sure to be better. And if it is, may I break the Shino?"

"A dangerous gamble."

After dinner, as she dexterously picked seeds

from the watermelon, Fumiko again pressed him to show her the bowl.

He sent the maid to open the tea cottage, and went out through the garden. He meant to bring the tea chest back with him, but Fumiko went along.

"I have no idea where it might be," he called back. "Kurimoto knows far better than I."

Fumiko was in the shadow of the blossom-heavy oleander. He could see, below the lowest of the white branches, stockinged feet in garden clogs.

The tea chest was in a cupboard at the side of the pantry.

Kikuji brought it into the main room and laid it before her. She knelt deferentially, as though waiting for him to untie the wrapping; but after a time she reached for it.

"If I may see it, then."

"It's a bit dusty." He took the chest by the wrapping and dusted it over the garden. "The pantry is alive with bugs, and there was a dead cicada in the cupboard."

"But this room is clean."

"Kurimoto cleaned it when she came to tell me that you and the Inamura girl were married. It was night, and she must have shut a cicada in the cupboard.

Taking out what appeared to be a tea bowl, Fumiko bent low to undo the sack. Her fingers trembled slightly.

The round shoulders were thrown forward, and to Kikuji, looking at her in profile, the long throat seemed even longer.

There was something engaging about the pouting lower lip, which pushed forward in proportion as the mouth was drawn earnestly shut, and about the plain swell of the ear lobes.

She looked up at him. "It's Karatsu." [1]

Kikuji came nearer.

"It's a very good bowl." She laid it on the floor matting.

It was a small, cylindrical Karatsu bowl, which, like the Shino, could be used for everyday.

"It's strong. Dignified—much better than the Shino."

"But can you compare Shino and Karatsu?"

"You can tell if you see them together."

Held by the power of the Karatsu, Kikuji took it on his knee and gazed at it.

"Shall I bring the Shino, then?"

"I'll get it." Fumiko stood up.

They put the Shino and the Karatsu side by side. Their eyes met, and fell to the bowls.

"A man's and a woman's." Kikuji spoke in some confusion. "When you see them side by side."

[1] A Kyūshū ware of Korean origin.

Fumiko nodded, as if unable to speak.

To Kikuji too the words had an odd ring.

The Karatsu was undecorated, greenish with a touch of saffron and a touch too of carmine. It swelled powerfully toward the base.

"A favorite your father took with him on trips. It's very much like your father."

Fumiko seemed not to sense the danger in the remark.

Kikuji could not bring himself to say that the Shino bowl was like her mother. But the two bowls before them were like the souls of his father and her mother.

The tea bowls, three or four hundred years old, were sound and healthy, and they called up no morbid thoughts. Life seemed to stretch taut over them, however, in a way that was almost sensual.

Seeing his father and Fumiko's mother in the bowls, Kikuji felt that they had raised two beautiful ghosts and placed them side by side.

The tea bowls were here, present, and the present reality of Kikuji and Fumiko, facing across the bowls, seemed immaculate too.

Kikuji had said to her, on the day after the seventh-day services for her mother, that there was something terrible in his being with her, facing her. Had the guilt and the fear been wiped away by the touch of the bowls?

"Beautiful," said Kikuji, as if to himself. "It wasn't Father's nature to play with tea bowls, and yet he did, and maybe they deadened his sense of guilt."

"I beg your pardon?"

"But when you see the bowl, you forget the defects of the old owner. Father's life was only a very small part of the life of a tea bowl."

"Death, waiting at your feet. I'm frightened. I've tried so many things. I've tried thinking that with death itself at my feet I can't be forever held by Mother's death."

"When you're held by the dead, you begin to feel that you aren't in this world yourself."

The maid came with a kettle and other tea utensils.

She had evidently concluded that, so long in the cottage, they needed water for tea.

Kikuji suggested to Fumiko that they use the Shino and the Karatsu here as if they themselves were on a trip.

Fumiko nodded simply. "May I use the Shino one last time before I break it?" She took the tea whisk from the box, and went to wash it.

The long summer day was still bright.

"As if on a trip," said Fumiko, twirling the small whisk in the small bowl.

"Off on a trip—and are we at an inn?"

"It doesn't have to be an inn. A river bank, or a mountain top. Maybe cold water would have been better, to make us think of the mountains." As she lifted the tea whisk, her near-black eyes rose and for an instant were on Kikuji. Then she looked down at the Karatsu, which she turned in the palm of one hand.

The eyes moved forward with the bowl, to a spot before Kikuji's knee.

He felt that she might come flowing over to him.

When she started to make tea in her mother's Shino, the whisk rustled against the bowl. She stopped.

"It's very hard."

"It must be hard in such a small bowl," said Kikuji. But the trouble was that Fumiko's hands were trembling.

Once she had stopped, there was no making the whisk move again.

Fumiko sat with bowed head, her eyes on her taut wrist.

"Mother won't let me."

"What!" Kikuji started up and took her by the shoulders, as if to pull her from the meshes of a curse.

There was no resistance.

· 4 ·

Unable to sleep, Kikuji waited for light through the cracks in the shutters, and went out to the cottage.

The broken Shino lay on the stepping stone before the stone basin.

He put together four large pieces to form a bowl. A piece large enough to admit his forefinger was missing from the rim.

Wondering if it might be somewhere on the ground, he started looking among the stones. Immediately he stopped.

He raised his eyes. A large star was shining through the trees to the east.

It was some years since he had last seen the morning star. He stood looking at it, and the sky began to cloud over.

The star was even larger, shining through the haze. The light was as if blurred by water.

It seemed dreary in contrast to the fresh glimmer of the star, to be hunting a broken bowl and trying to put it together.

He threw the pieces down again.

The evening before, Fumiko had flung the Shino against the basin before he could stop her.

He had cried out.

But he had not looked for the pieces in the shadows among the stones. He had rather put his arm around Fumiko, supporting her. As she fell forward in the act of throwing the Shino, she seemed herself about to collapse against the basin.

"There is much better Shino," she murmured.

Was she still sad at the thought of having Kikuji compare it with better Shino?

He lay sleepless, and an echo of her words came to him, more poignantly clean in remembrance.

Waiting for daylight, he went out to look for the pieces.

Then, seeing the star, he threw them down again.

And looking up, he cried out.

There was no star. In the brief moment when his eyes were on the discarded pieces, the morning star had disappeared in the clouds.

He gazed at the eastern sky for a time, as if to retrieve something stolen.

The clouds would not be heavy; but he could not tell where the star was. The clouds broke near the horizon. The faint red deepened where they touched the roofs of houses.

"I can't just leave it," he said aloud. He picked up the pieces again, and put them in the sleeve of his night kimono.

It would be sad to leave them there. And besides, Kurimoto Chikako might come calling.

He thought of burying the bowl beside the stone basin, because Fumiko had broken it there in such obvious desperation. Instead, he wrapped the pieces in paper, put them in a drawer, and went back to bed.

What had she so dreaded having him compare the Shino with?

And why had the possibility so worried her? Kikuji could think of no reason.

Now, even more than the evening before, he could think of no one with whom to compare her.

She had become absolute, beyond comparison. She had become decision and fate.

Always before, she had been Mrs. Ota's daughter. Now, he had forgotten—the idea had quite left him that the mother's body was in a subtle way transferred to the daughter, to lure him into strange fantasies.

He had at length made his way outside the dark, ugly curtain.

Had the breach in her cleanness rescued him?

There had been no resistance from Fumiko, only from the cleanness itself.

That fact, one might think, told how deep he had sunk into the meshes of the curse, how complete the paralysis was; but Kikuji felt the reverse, that he had escaped the curse and the paralysis. It was as if an addict had been freed of his addiction by taking the ultimate dose of a drug.

Kikuji called Fumiko from his office. She worked for a wool wholesaler in Kanda.

She was not at work. Kikuji had left home sleepless. Had Fumiko fallen into a deep sleep at perhaps dawn? Or, in her shame, had she shut herself up for the day?

In the afternoon she still was not at work, and he asked where she lived.

Her new address would have been on the letter yesterday; but Fumiko had torn it up envelope and all and put the pieces in her pocket. At dinner they had talked of her work, and he remembered the name of the firm. He had not asked where she lived. It had been as if her dwelling were Kikuji himself.

On his way home, he looked for the rooming house. It was behind Ueno Park.

Fumiko was not there.

A girl twelve or thirteen, just back from school to judge from her student uniform, came to the door and went inside again.

"Miss Ota is out. She said she was going away with a friend."

"Away? She went on a trip? What time was it? And where did she say she was going?"

The girl went inside again, and this time she did not come to the door. "I really don't know. Mother is out." She seemed afraid of Kikuji. She had thin eyebrows.

Kikuji looked back as he went out the gate, but he could not tell which was Fumiko's room. It was a fairly decent two-storey house with a little garden.

She had said that death was at her feet. Kikuji's own feet were suddenly cold.

He wiped his face with his handkerchief. The blood seemed to leave as he wiped, and he wiped more violently. The handkerchief was wet and dark. He felt a cold sweat at his back.

"She has no reason to die," he muttered.

There was no reason for Fumiko to die, Fumiko who had brought him to life.

But had the simple directness of the evening before been the directness of death?

Was she, like her mother, guilt-ridden, afraid of the directness?

"And only Kurimoto is left." As if spitting out all the accumulated venom on the woman he took for his enemy, Kikuji hurried into the shade of the park.

A NOTE ABOUT THE AUTHOR

YASUNARI KAWABATA *was one of Japan's most distinguished novelists. He is famous for adding to the once fashionable naturalism imported from France a sensual, more Japanese impressionism. He was born in Osaka in 1899. As a boy, he hoped to become a painter, an aspiration later reflected in his novels. But his first stories were published while he was still in high school, and he decided to become a writer.*

He was graduated from Tokyo Imperial University in 1924. His story "The Izu Dancer," first published in 1925, and recently republished by the Charles E. Tuttle Company, appeared in the Atlantic Monthly *in 1954. It captures the shy eroticism of adolescence, and thereafter Kawabata devoted his novels largely to aspects of love.* SNOW COUNTRY, *a novel concerning the love affair of a Tokyo snob with a country geisha, was published in English in 1956 and excited much praise.*

Kawabata was also a prominent literary critic and discovered and sponsored such remarkable young writers as Yukio Mishima. In 1948 he was appointed chairman of the Japanese Center of the P.E.N. Club. His death by suicide in April 1972 was a tremendous shock to his admirers both in Japan and abroad.

Other Titles in the Tuttle Library